Edwin Simpson

The dramatic unities

Third Edition

Edwin Simpson

The dramatic unities
Third Edition

ISBN/EAN: 9783337303907

Printed in Europe, USA, Canada, Australia, Japan

Cover: Foto ©Andreas Hilbeck / pixelio.de

More available books at **www.hansebooks.com**

THE

DRAMATIC UNITIES.

BY

EDWIN SIMPSON-BAIKIE.

THIRD EDITION.

LONDON:
TRÜBNER & CO., LUDGATE HILL.
1878.

PRINTED BY BALLANTYNE AND COMPANY
EDINBURGH AND LONDON.

PREFACE TO SECOND EDITION.

———

THE notices which up to this time have appeared of this little book have praised it far beyond its merits; and the writer can only, in modest wonderment, cordially thank those critics who have so over-appreciated his efforts to throw a little light on the history of the dramatic unities. The *Athenæum* reviewer, indeed, seems to think that the work was superfluous; that the unities had, in England at least, already been disposed of and laid to rest. If this be so, no one can have greater cause for satisfaction than the present writer. The only object of this essay was to show that the unities are not only useless, but absolutely prejudicial and detrimental to the dramatic art; and that, consequently, the writer for the stage ought to be bound by no other rules than the ordinary ones of good taste, probability, and common sense.

PREFACE TO FIRST EDITION.

THE following pages have been suggested by an apparent inclination on the part of some of our leading dramatic critics to revive the old doctrine of the unities of time and place. As it is of importance to present and future dramatists to know whether they are expected to work in accordance with these unities, it is hoped that this short compilation of authorities on the subject may be found useful, and contribute, in some measure, towards a settlement of the question.

I.

THE ORIGIN OF THE UNITIES.

THE dramatic unities took their rise at the court of Leo the Tenth, and may be ascribed indirectly to the impulse given there to the study and imitation of classical literature. *Directly, however,* their invention, or revival, is traceable to one of the most gifted members of that gifted assemblage, namely, Gian Giorgio Trissino. Roscoe, in his " Life of Leo the Tenth," says—

" Although the study of the ancient languages had long been revived in Italy, yet no idea seems to have been entertained before the time of Leo X. of improving the style of Italian composition by a closer adherence to the regularity and purity **of** the Greek and Roman writers. Some efforts had indeed been made to transfuse the spirit, **or** at least the sense, of these productions into the Italian tongue. The 'Metamorphoses' of Ovid, and the ' Æneid ' of the Momtuan bard, had thus been translated into prose ; and the 'Thebaid' of Statius, the 'Phar-

salia' of Lucan, and the 'Satires' of Juvenal,
with some detached parts of the writings of Ovid
and Virgil, had been translated into Italian verse ;
but in so rude and unskilful a manner, as to produce,
like a bad mirror, rather a caricature than a resem-
blance. As the Italian scholars became more inti-
mately acquainted with the works of the ancients,
they began to feel the influence of their taste, and
to imbibe some portion of their spirit. No longer
satisfied with the humble and laborious task of
translating these authors, they, with a laudable
simulation, endeavoured to rival the boasted remains
of ancient genius by productions of a similar kind
in their native tongue. . . . The person who is
entitled to the chief credit of having formed, and in
some degree executed, this design, is the learned
Gian Giorgio Trissino."—(Chap. xvi.)

Of Trissino himself, Sismondi says—

" Born at Vicenza in 1478 of an illustrious family,
he was equally qualified by his education for letters
and for public business. He came to Rome when
he was twenty-four years of age, and had resided
there a considerable time, when Pope Leo X., struck
by his talents, sent him as ambassador to the
Emperor Maximilian. Under the pontificate of
Clement VII., he was also charged with embassies
to Charles V., and to the Republic of Venice, and
was decorated by the former with the order of the

Golden Fleece. In **the** midst of public affairs **he** cultivated **with** ardour poetry and the languages. He was rich, and possessing a fine taste in architecture, he employed Palladio to erect a country-house in the **best** style at Criccoli. He died in 1550, aged seventy-two."—(Literature of the Italians, xv.)

Besides his once celebrated poem on " Italia Liberata," in which he was the first to introduce the *versi sciolti*, or blank verse of the Italian language, he composed a poem entitled " La Poetica," probably founded on the " Poeticon " of Aristotle ; and it was no doubt this work which suggested **to** him the idea of writing **a** tragedy in accordance with **the unities. This** was his **" Sofonisba,"** produced in the year 1515, and the first dramatic piece in which the rules of Aristotle were strictly observed. Of this Sismondi says—

" The most just title to fame possessed by Trissino is founded on his ' Sofonisba,' which may **be considered** as the first regular tragedy since the revival of letters, and which we may, with still greater justice, regard as the last of the tragedies of antiquity, **so** exactly **is** it founded on the **principles** of the Grecian **dramas, and,** above all, on those of Euripides."—(Literature **of the** Italians, **xv.**)

So close an imitation, indeed, was his piece of **the** Greek drama, that the **usual** division into acts **and** scenes was omitted, and **a** chorus introduced.

Rucellai presently succeeded his friend Trissino as
an imitator of the ancient Greek drama, and was
followed by numerous others, all of whom wrote in
accordance with the unities. In fact, from the
time of Trissino, the rules of classical tragedy were
firmly established in Italy, and held undisputed
sway for the next three centuries. The works, however, of his immediate followers, however correct
in their imitation of the classical drama, were not
destined to live beyond their own immediate time.

"The early Italian drama," says Sismondi,
"comprises a considerable number of pieces. But
the pedantry which gave them birth deprived them
from their cradle of all originality and of all real
feeling. The action and the representation, of which
the dramatic poet should never for an instant lose
sight, are constantly neglected; and philosophy
and erudition usurp the place of the emotion
necessary to the scene. . . . Even the names of the
dramatic pieces in Italy, in the sixteenth century,
are scarcely preserved in the records of literature.
. . . These pretended restorers of the theatre conformed, it is true, to all the precepts of Aristotle
from the time of the sixteenth century, and to the
rules of classical poetry even before their authority
was proclaimed; but this avails little when they
are wanting in life and interest. We cannot read
these tragedies without insufferable fatigue; and it

is difficult to form an idea of the patience of **the** spectators condemned to listen to these long decla- mations and tedious dialogues, usurping the place of action, which ought to be brought before their eyes."—(Literature of the Italians, xv.)

It was probably owing to the feebleness of these productions, and the little interest **they** excited abroad, that more than a century passed before the unities made their way into France. When they, in course of time, did so, it was by means of the same piece which had served to introduce them on the Italian stage. Trissino's " Sofonisba " was tran- slated **by** one Mairet, and produced at Rouen in **the** year 1629.

" An author," says **Voltaire, "named** Mairet **was** the first who, in his imitation of Trissino's 'Sophonisba,' introduced the rule of the three uni- **ties,** which you " (the Italians) " had taken from the Greeks." * **(1)**

And again—

" Mairet's ' Sophonisba' was the first piece **in** France where the three unities appeared." **(2)**

In another place he adds—

" It is true that the ' Sophonisba ' **of** Mairet had a merit which was then entirely new in France,— that of being in accordance with the rules of **the**

---

* The original passages are given in the Appendix.

theatre. **The three unities** of action, time, and place are there strictly observed, **and the author was** regarded as the father of the French stage." **(3)**

This is confirmed by Laharpe, who says—

" ' Sophonisba,' imitated from the play of that name **by Trissino, was the** first of our tragedies constructed upon a regular plan, **and** subjected to the three unities." **(4)**

These new rules, **strict as they were,** seem to have been immediately received **with** great favour in France. On Corneille, who had produced his first piece (" Mélite") in the same year in which " Sophonisba" was produced, they seem to have made a great impression. He became their vigorous supporter and exponent ; and in all his pieces, from the " Cid " (produced in 1636) to " Surena " (1674), he made honest, **but not** always successful, efforts to keep within the prescribed limits of time and place. In 1656 he published his " Trois Discours," **the** last of which is an earnest argument in favour of **the** use and the necessity of the unities. Followed by Racine, and later by Voltaire, Corneille's principles became a law which it **was** looked upon as a heresy to doubt, and to which **all** French writers **for the** stage were bound to submit themselves. **It is true** that in the early part of **the** eighteenth **century** the unities were vigorously **attacked by a** writer named **De** la Motte, but against **such** a powerful adversary as Voltaire, he had little chance of seeing his opinions succeed; and, indeed, his defeat only served to strengthen the champions of " regularity."

"One must," says Corneille, "observe the unities of action, time, and place; there can be no doubt about that." (5)

And Voltaire, writing in 1730, says—

"All nations begin to regard as barbarous those times when even the greatest geniuses, such as Lopez de Vega and Shakespeare, were ignorant of this system; and they even confess the obligation they are under to us for having rescued them from this barbarism. . . . Even if I had no other answer to give M. de la Motte than the fact that Corneille, Racine, Molière, Addison, Congreve, and Maffei have all observed the laws of the stage, that ought to be enough to restrain any one who should entertain the idea of violating them." (6)

For two hundred years then, from the time of Corneille to that of Victor Hugo, the unities reigned supreme in France, and were only finally overthrown on the production of the latter writer's " Hernani," in the year 1830.

Of the dramatic unities themselves, those of action and time are founded upon passages in Aristotle's " Poeticon," and that of place on what was considered to be the usual practice of the Greek dramatists. The unity of action can scarcely be defined in a few words, and the various interpretations put upon it will be given later. In their original form, the unity of time demanded that the action should take place within twenty-four hours, "or exceed them but little;" while the unity of place required that the scene should not be transferred beyond the bounds of the palace or dwelling where the action was supposed to occur. This unity of place, as will be seen, has been subjected to various modifications, and is apparently, in the present day, chiefly understood to mean that no change of scene is allowable within the limits of an act. This, however, will be discussed in its proper place, and we need not refer to it at length here. It may be observed *en passant,* that, as may be supposed, the student will look in vain for any allusion to the unities in the "Ars Poetica" of Horace, unless indeed the following passage may be pressed into the service of the unity of action :—

> "Si quid inexpertum scenæ committis, et audes
> Personam formare novam ; servetur ad imum
> Qualis ab incepto processerit, et sibi constet."

II.

THE UNITY OF ACTION.

THE passages in the " Poeticon " of Aristotle from which the unity of action is derived are as follows :—

" Tragedy, then, **is** the imitation of a grave and complete **action** possessing magnitude; (clothed) in pleasing language, independently of the (pleasurable) ideas (suggested) in its other parts; set forth by means of persons acting, and not by means of narration; and through pity and fear effecting the purification of those passions. . . . The most important, however, of these (requisites) is the setting together of the incidents."—(vi.) (7)

" It will then **be** granted that tragedy **is** the imitation of **a** perfect and complete action, possessing magnitude; for there may be a whole which has no magnitude. But a whole **is** that which has a beginning, **a** middle, and an **end.** The beginning is that which, of necessity, follows nothing else, but after which something is bound **to** be, or to be produced. The end, on the contrary, is that which naturally comes after something else, either necessarily or for the most part, but after which there is nothing else. The middle, however, is that both before and after which there is something else. It is necessary, then, that well-combined fables should neither begin whence, nor end where, chance may dictate, but should be composed according to the above-mentioned forms."—(vii.)

"It is fit, then, that—just as in other imitative arts, the imitation is the imitation of one single thing—the story also, since it is the imitation of an action, should be that of one whole and complete action; and that the parts of the transactions should be so combined that, any of them being either transposed or taken away, the whole would become different and disturbed."—(viii.)

Various interpretations have been placed on these passages, the most important of which we subjoin. Corneille says—

"I maintain, then, that the unity of action consists, in comedy, in the unity of the intrigue, or of the obstacles offered to the designs of the principal personages; in tragedy, in the unity of peril, whether it be that the hero sinks under it, or extricates himself from it. I do not, of course, maintain that it is not allowable to admit several perils in the one, and several intrigues or obstacles in the other, provided that, in freeing himself from the one, the personage falls of necessity into **the** other." (8)

Voltaire, in his remarks on this passage, says—

" We think that Corneille here understands, by **unity of** action and of intrigue, a principal action, to which the various interests and the private intrigues **are** subordinate, forming a whole composed of several parts, which all of them tend to the same object." (9)

A little further on, however, we find some remarks which are not quite so clear—

" Corneille is quite right when he says that there ought to be **only** one complete action. **We** doubt, **however, whether** one can gain this object otherwise than by means of several imperfect actions." (10)

Laharpe, with, probably, some reminiscence of the passage in Horace already quoted, understands the unity of action to lie in the consistency of the characters.

" Aristotle desires—and all the legislators **on** the subject have followed him in this—that a character **be** the same at the conclusion as at the commencement." (11)

Lessing, otherwise a bitter enemy of the unities, speaks with respect of Aristotle's views on this subject.

"There is nothing," he says, "that Aristotle has more strongly recommended to the poet than the proper composition of his story. . . . He defines the story as the imitation of an action, and the action is, in his opinion, the connection of the incidents. The action is the whole, the incidents are the component parts of the whole ; and as the excellence of any complete whole depends upon the excellence of its several parts and their combination, so also is a tragic action more or less perfect in proportion as the incidents—each for itself, and all conjointly—are in harmony with the purposes of the tragedy." (12)

Schlegel says—

" Far, therefore, from rejecting the law of a perfect unity in tragedy as unnecessary, I require a deeper, more intrinsic, and more mysterious unity than that with which most critics are satisfied. This unity I find in the tragic compositions of Shakespeare, in quite as great perfection as in those of Æschylus and Sophocles. I miss it, on the contrary, in many of those tragedies which are accounted correct by critics of a dissecting turn of mind. Logical coherence, the casual connection, I hold to be equally essential to tragedy and every serious drama." (13)

However, then, we may interpret these passages, there is nothing to which we can take exception.

If they mean that a dramatic piece should consist of
a clear story, clearly told, and with a fixed and distinct purpose running through it from beginning to
end, every one **will** agree **on** that point. It will
also **be readily** granted **that the less** important
actions of the piece should **be** subordinate **to, and
not** overpower the interest of, the main thread **of
the** story. As to the consistency of the characters,
allowing that the unity of time is beneficial, **there**
can be no objections to Laharpe's opinion. It
would be unnatural to allow **a** personage suddenly
to change his character within the twenty-four
hours. **To** represent him **as** supremely good in the
morning, **and** violently wicked in the evening, would
tax the laws of probability **too far.** Granting, then,
the unity of time, it would seem to be only right, and
even necessary, that a personage should, within the
period of a day, be required to preserve his consistency of character. The principle **of** the unity of
action, then, may be allowed to be not only harmless, but even beneficial. **It is** of comparatively
little importance in comparison with those of time
and place; and while the one has been allowed to
sleep in peace, over the other two angry contests
have raged, and bitter battles have been fought, until
quite recent times.

III.

THE UNITY OF TIME.

THE unity of time has for its authority the following passage of the " Poeticon:"—

"Moreover, (the epos differs from tragedy) as regards length; for the latter attempts, as far as possible, to restrict itself to a single revolution of the sun, or to exceed it but little; whereas the epos is indefinite as regards time, and in this respect differs (from tragedy)." (14)

But the unities had scarcely begun to gain ground in France, before we find Corneille pleading for an extension of this limit. Writing in 1636, he says—

"For my part, I find that there are subjects so difficult to confine within the limits of so short a time, that not only would I allow them the full twenty-four hours, but I would even take advantage of the liberty accorded by the philosopher to exceed them in some measure, and would without hesitation go as far as thirty hours." (15)

Voltaire, however, in his note to this, objects to going beyond the twenty-four hours.

"The unity of time," he says, " is founded not only on the laws of Aristotle, but on those of nature. It would, in fact, be extremely proper that the action should not extend beyond the time required for representation. . . . It is clear, however, that this merit may be sacrificed to a much greater one, which is that of interesting the audience. If you can cause more tears to flow by extending your action to twenty-four hours, then take a day and a night, but do not go beyond that. In the latter case, the illusion would be too much impaired." (16)

Corneille had no followers in his attempt, and the hard and fast rule of a day and a night was universally accepted by the French dramatists. Schlegel, however, considers that Aristotle, in the above passage, had no intention of laying down a fixed and absolute law, but was merely mentioning what he had noticed as a usual practice of the Greek writers. To this practice, as we shall see presently, there are some very notable exceptions ; but granting that, in the majority of instances, the action of a Greek drama could be made to pass within the twenty-four hours, it is doubtful whether this took place in obedience to any known canon or precept. It is at least possible that the peculiarity arose from the structure of their pieces, the simple

action of which could easily be supposed to pass
within that time. Of plot, in our sense of the word,
there is little. No incidents or events of any kind
are allowed to disturb the foregone conclusion as to
the fate of the principal personage. From the beginning to the end, he is the victim of an in-
exorable and unavoidable destiny. The spectators
know from the commencement the fate which
awaits him, and, in most cases, nothing is allowed
to modify or alter the inevitable decree. In some
dramas the conclusion is announced in the first
hundred lines of the play—either that the victim
will have to undergo his prescribed fate, or that
some god or goddess has taken him under protection, and will deliver him from it. Another
thing which adds to the simplicity of the old Greek
plots is the fact that love or passion, as understood
in modern times, plays no part in their pieces.
The relations of the sexes, with all the wonderful
complications which spring from them in our day,
were things which caused no trouble among the
Greeks. A Greek woman lived a life of seclusion
as a girl, and lived a life of seclusion as a wife.
When the time came for her to be married, a bride-
groom was procured, and her marriage ordered and
arranged, and imposed upon her by her parents. (17)

"Are you then, father," says Iphigenia, "going to
remove me to the dwelling of another?"

" Be still," replies Agamemnon, "it is not becoming for a girl to know such things."

A Greek woman then was simply transferred
from the *gynæceum* of her father to that of her
husband ; and outside those walls she could have no
cares and no interests—unless, indeed, of an illicit
kind. Being then free from all the disturbing
elements of love, a Greek tragedy could move on
from the beginning to the end in its own simple
and dignified manner. It is true that the " Hippolytus" of Euripides turns upon the passion of
" Phœdra" for her stepson Hippolytus ; but this
passion, as announced by Venus in the opening lines
of the play, is only inspired by that goddess as a
means of punishing Hippolytus for his neglect of
her and exclusive worship of Diana. The first
mistake, then, made by the French, was that of
applying to their own pieces rules intended for the
regulation of a drama, which proceeded from a
totally different form of religion, and totally different conditions of society.

But let us now examine the unity of time, as it
actually exists in the Greek plays. Some stress is
laid by Schlegel on the argument that the rule as
regards time ought to apply to the whole trilogy—
or series of three plays—and not to each of its parts.
It will be remembered that no Greek play was ever
performed separately. The whole three pieces

B

forming the trilogy were performed on the same
day, and immediately following each other. Schlegel,
then, would have us consider the separate plays as
something analogous to our acts—not complete in
themselves, but as only forming part of a whole.
This theory, however, seems scarcely maintainable,
from the fact that Aristotle could never have meant
that the events of the whole trilogy were to pass
within the twenty-four hours.   Let us take the
" Oresteia " of Æschylus, consisting of the " Agamemnon," the " Coephori," and the " Eumenides,"
as the only perfect example of a Greek trilogy we
have received. The story in each case consists of
some striking event in the life of one person, or in
that of some member of his family. In the
" Agamemnon " we have the return of Agamemnon from Troy, and his murder, and that of
Cassandra, by Clytemnestra. In the " Coephori "
this murder of his father is revenged on his mother,
and her lover Ægisthus, by Orestes. In the "Eumenides " we have Orestes pursued by the Furies for
this matricide, and ultimately, under Apollo's
protection, acquitted by the Areopagus.   Take,
again, the "Œdipus Tyrannus" and " Coloneus" of
Sophocles, both of which would appear to belong
to the same trilogy. In the first we have an
account of his solution of the Sphinx's riddle, his
marriage to Jocasta, who is subsequently found to

be his mother, his horror at this discovery, and consequent mutilation of his eyes. In the " Coloneus " we find him in Athens, having been banished from Thebes. An attempt is made to induce him to return to Thebes, but he refuses to do so, and is carried off to the shades in a fearful storm. Now **in all** these plays, except the " Eumenides "—of which we shall speak presently—the action may very easily be supposed to pass within twenty-four hours ; but not so the whole trilogy. Between the pieces there are, as Schlegel says, " gaps of time as considerable as those between the acts of many a Spanish drama." This is evident when we remember that, for instance, **in the** interval between the " Agamemnon " and **the** "Coephori," Orestes grows up from childhood to manhood. In that between the "Coephori" and the "Eumenides," he has to perform the journey from Mycenæ to Delphi. The same may be said of the " Œdipus Tyrannus " and " Coloneus ; " for in the interval between the two, not only does Œdipus go from Thebes to Athens, but Antigone would seem to have grown up from a child to a woman. It is evident, then, we think, that when Aristotle laid down his rule of twenty-four hours, he intended it to apply to the separate pieces of the trilogy, and not to the whole.

Another question, however, presents itself in

considering the "Oresteia," and that is, what object
could the Greek dramatists have had in limiting
themselves to the space of twenty-four hours? As
we know, the people went to the theatre at day-
break, and remained there till sunset. The performance lasted the whole day, and during this time,
we are told, three trilogies and an after-piece were
represented. Supposing, then, that each piece dealt
with the occurrences of a day, and each trilogy, consequently, with those of three days, we should thus
have the events of nine or ten days presented in
succession. But why this particular number? or
rather, why should the dramatists have been restricted
to one day, when the events of ten days were represented at the same performance? If the imagina-
tions of the spectators could grasp the events of ten
days presented in rapid succession, surely they
would have been able to realise those of twelve, or
fifteen, or twenty, or more.

But let us now see how far the Greek dramatists
themselves observed the unity of time. On this
subject, Schlegel has the following remarks :—

"But, it will be objected, the ancient tragic
writers, at least, observed the unity of time. This
expression is altogether inappropriate. It should be
the identity of the real time with that represented ;
but even then it will not apply to the ancients.
What they observed is nothing but the *apparent*

continuity of time. **It is of** importance to attend to
this distinction, the *apparent*, for they undoubtedly
allow much more to take place during the choral odes
than could really happen within their actual duration.
In the 'Agamemnon' of Æschylus the whole
interval from the destruction of Troy to his **arrival
at** Mycenæ is included, which evidently must have
consisted of a considerable number of days. In
the ' Trachiniæ ' of Sophocles, during the course **of**
the piece the voyage from Thessaly to Eubœa is
thrice performed. And again, in the ' Suppliants '
of Euripides, during a single choral ode the entire
march of an army from Athens **to** Thebes **is**
supposed to **take** place, **a** battle to **be** fought, and
the general to return victorious. **So far** were the
Greeks above this sort of anxious calculation. They
had, however, a particular reason for observing the
apparent continuity of time, and that was the constant presence of the chorus. When the latter leaves
the stage, the continuous progress is interrupted,
as in the striking instance in the 'Eumenides'
of Æschylus, where the whole interval **is omitted**
which was required **for** Orestes to **proceed from**
Delphi to Athens." **(18)**

Again, in the **"Andromache,"** Orestes and
Hermione perform the journey from Phthia in
Thessaly to Delphi. Not only this, but a messenger
returns from there, bearing news of their **arrival, and**

of the murder of Neoptolemus. All this takes
place without any break in the action of the piece.
In the " Heraclidæ," in the early part of the piece,
the herald of the King of Argos departs from
Athens threatening him. Before the conclusion of
the piece the Argive army has arrived, fights a
battle, and is defeated. In the " Iphigenia in
Tauris," Iphigenia, in company with Orestes and
Pylades, escaping from Tauri, reaches the seashore,
embarks for the purpose of making their escape, and
is driven back by stress of weather. In the
" Alcestis," that lady and Hercules descend to and
return from the lower regions during the course of
the piece, but it is true that that journey may not
have required any very long time for its accomplishment.

From these instances we see, then, that even the
letter of the unity of time was frequently violated
by the Greek dramatists; its spirit was still more
often infringed. Events bearing upon the action of
the piece, and requiring a considerable time to
happen, are related either by the chorus, a messenger,
a herald, or a servant. Most of the Greek dramas,
and nearly all those of Euripides, are preceded by a
long statement for the purpose of clearing the
ground for the commencement of the story. Thus
it happens that many events, a portion of which
should have been presented to the eyes of the spec-

tators, are merely related by word **of mouth.** **That**
this was done to save the unity of **time appears**
improbable, for it is not saving it, it is only evading
it. One reason might have been the desire on the
part of the dramatist to restrict the number of his
characters as much as possible. We know that
Æschylus was the first to add a second actor; and it
may be that public opinion, even in the time of
Sophocles and Euripides, looked upon it as a merit
in the dramatist to employ as few personages as
possible.

But if we turn to the French stage, we find their
writers, from the very **first,** moving extremely **un-**
easily in their new fetters. "**The** unities must **be**
observed, there can be no doubt about that," says
Corneille, "but we must have the thirty hours."
Even with this extension, Corneille could not make
his practice accord with his theory. In the "Cid,"
for instance, we have the following events. The
father of the heroine gives the father of the hero a
box on the ear. He is, therefore, challenged to a
duel by the hero, and killed. The heroine, although
still loving him, demands his life from the king, who
orders him to join the campaign against the Moors.
From this he returns victorious, having performed
prodigies of valour, and taken prisoners two of the
hostile kings. The heroine still demands his life,
upon which he is ordered to meet in single combat

another lover of the heroine, and on condition that she shall become the wife of the conqueror. In this he is again successful, having disarmed his adversary and spared his life, when the heroine at last agrees to forgive him. The hero thus goes through a campaign, two duels, and several love-scenes, all in the space of twenty-four hours. Corneille, however, pathetically admits that "the rule of twenty-four hours presses rather too hard on the incidents of the piece, and that the Cid had well deserved two or three days of rest after his campaign, before being called upon to fight another duel. He is also willing to admit that the second demand of the heroine for justice comes rather too soon after the first one, and that, in fact, fiction would have allowed seven or eight days to intervene. "But there," he says, "you see the inconvenience of the rule." ("Examen du Cid"). There is something almost touching in the sight of Corneille's genius chafing under these petty bonds. The anxiety with which, in his "Examen," prefixed to each play, he tries to persuade the reader that the unities are preserved, is half pitiable, half comical. Thus, of "Horace," he remarks that the action is not too hurried, and there is nothing improbable in its passing within the given time. In "Cinna," the unity of time is not incommoded by the necessities of representation. About "Polyencte" there are serious difficulties.

"When a king grants amnesties, or performs other acts of clemency, his orders are seldom carried out on the same day. However, by a slight stretch of the imagination, the doubts of a good-natured auditor will disappear easily enough." As to "Pompée," "it has been necessary to change into a mere rising of the people a war which could not have lasted less than a year, seeing that, soon after Cæsar's departure from Alexandria, Cleopatra gave birth to Cæsarion." In the "Menteur" the unity of time is not strained, provided you allow the full four and twenty hours. In his other pieces, "Rodogune," "Heraclius," "Don Sanche d' Aragon," and "Nicomède," it is satisfactory to find that everything is right as regards time, but the unity of place still continues to give trouble.

In fact, on reading over any of the tragedies of Corneille, Racine, or Voltaire, the extreme improbability of such a series of events occurring in one day strikes us at once. We are continually reminded of the judgment passed by the Academy on "The Cid."—"The poet, in endeavouring to observe the rules of art, has chosen rather to sin against those of nature." And this remark will apply to nearly all the so-called "regular tragedies." It is in some cases possible that the events presented might happen in one day, but very unlikely that they should.

We have, for instance, conspiracies formed and
carried out on the same day; persons passing from
the extremes of love to those of jealousy, and back
again, all on the same day; battles fought, and the
hero returning victorious on the same day; messengers going long distances, and the effect of their
message being known at the place from which
they started on the same day; and finally, pro-
posals of marriage made, the preparations completed,
and the wedding either taking place or being pre-
vented, all on the same day. Look at the succession of occurrences in Voltaire's "Zaire." At the
commencement of the piece the heroine makes a
confession of love for Orosmane, at the same time
stating that she has no intention of becoming his
mistress. Later, Orosmane offers her his hand, and
the marriage festivities are ordered and prepared.
Zaire then discovers her father in the person of one
of Orosmane's prisoners, and also the fact that she
is a Christian. (It is *apropos* of this fact, that the
curious line occurs which is put into the mouth of
Zaire. On being reminded of it, " Pourquoi me
rappeler mes ennuis?" answers the ingenuous
maiden.) In accordance, then, with the wishes of
her father, she refuses to proceed to the marriage
ceremony, without, however, giving Orosmane her
real reasons. We are still only in the third act, so
the wedding preparations must have required but a

very short time to complete. In the end, Orosmane attributes her refusal to infidelity, and discovering her in the company of a newly-found **brother,** he stabs her. Surely this **is a** startling series of events to occur within the space of one day.

As to the same author's " Merope," Lessing shall speak of that.

" It is true," he says, " that these writers pride themselves on the most scrupulous ' regularity ; ' but it is also they who either put so wide a construction upon their rules, that it is scarcely worth while to call them rules at all, or they observe them in such **an** awkward and constrained manner, that it gives one a greater shock to see them so observed, than if **they** did not observe **them at all.** (19)

" Now, let any man just consider the events which he (Voltaire) causes to happen in one day, and then say how many absurdities he will have to picture to himself. Let him take the fullest possible day ; let him take the thirty hours which Corneille allows. It is true that I see no physical obstacles to hinder all the incidents taking place within this time, but I see all the more moral ones. It is certainly not absolutely impossible that a man may propose for the hand of **a** woman, and be married to her within the twelve hours—especially when he has the power of dragging her by force before the **priest.** But when such **a** thing happens, surely

we have the right to demand the most forcible and pressing reasons for such extremely violent haste. When, however, we find not a shadow of these reasons, how shall that which is only just physically possible be made probable to us." Then follows a long description of the events in "Merope," and the absurdity of causing them to pass in one day. He then proceeds—

"Of what use is it to the poet that the incidents of each act, supposing them really to happen, should not occupy more time than the performance of the act really demands; and that this time, together with that allowed for the pauses, should not even extend to a full revolution of the sun? Is he on that account supposed to have observed the unity of time? To the words of the rule he has kept, but not to the spirit of it; for that which he causes to be done in one day may perhaps be done in one day, but no sensible man would do it in that time. The physical unity of time is not enough; the moral unity must be there too. For the violation of the last is sensible to all; whereas the violation of the first, even although it should involve an improbability, is not, on the whole, so offensive, because by many the improbability will remain unobserved." (20)

It was in this way, then, that the French dramatists conformed to those unities which they vio-

lently protested to be necessary to every well-
constructed tragedy. Voltaire himself, the inde-
fatigable champion of the unities, and to whom
Hamlet was a "coarse and barbarous piece, relieved
by some traits of genius," was, of all others, the
greatest offender in this respect. He proclaimed
loudly the necessity of the unity of time, and, in
almost every case, either violated it or evaded it.
That he, in common with Corneille and Racine,
was sincerely anxious to observe the rule, there can
be no doubt. That they honestly and earnestly
tried to do so, is certain. If, then, the difficulty
was so great that they could only observe it by
evading it, the reflection at once suggests itself, Or
what use is the rule?

That the rule regarding time is of no advantage
to the dramatist—that it not only does not assist
him, but actually impedes him in the execution of
his work—will, we think, have been sufficiently
shown from the above instances. Let us now
inquire whether the laws of probability demand
that the dramatist should be tied down to such a
rule in the interest of the spectators. It is clear
that the unity of time is founded upon the assump-
tion, that to present on the stage a succession of
occurrences which require more than twenty-four
hours for their accomplishment involves an improbability. In other words, that the imagination

is unable to follow, or refuses to realise, a longer chain of events, when submitted to it in rapid succession. But is this so? Let us first take Schlegel's opinion on the subject.

"Corneille, with reason, finds this rule extremely inconvenient. He therefore prefers the most lenient interpretation of it, and says that he would, without the slightest scruple, extend the duration of the action to thirty hours. Others, however, insist on the hard and fast rule that the action should occupy no longer a time than that required for its representation—that is to say, from two to three hours. The dramatic poet, they demand, must be a man who is always punctual to his hour. On the whole, the latter show a better case than the more indulgent critics. For the only basis of the rule can be the observance of a probability supposed to be necessary to the illusion, namely, that the time represented should agree with the real time. If we once allow a difference between the two, such as that between two hours and thirty hours, we may with perfect right go farther. The conception of illusion has caused great mistakes in theories of art. It has often been understood to consist in that mistaken idea, that that which is represented is reality. Were this so, the terrors of tragedy would be a real torture, a load, like the pressure of an Alpine mountain, upon the imagination. No, theatrical illusion, like every other poetical one, **is a** waking dream, **to** which we voluntarily surrender ourselves. To produce it, writer and actor must powerfully work upon the imagination; the calculation of probabilities can give no assistance. This demand of literal deception, pushed to the extreme, would make all poetical form impossible; for we know very well **that** mythological and historical personages were not **in** the habit of speaking our language, that impassioned grief does not express itself in verse, &c. What an unpoetical spectator must that one be, who, instead of following in a sympathetic manner the incidents **of the piece,** were **to sit,** watch in **hand, like a prison** warder, counting out **to the** heroes of the tragedy **the** minutes they still had to live and act! Is, then, our soul a clockwork which tells the hours and the minutes with infallible accuracy? and has it not rather a quite distinct mode of reckoning the hours of amusement and those of ennui? In the former, time passes quickly; in the latter, when we feel all our powers clogged, it grows to something quite immeasurable. So it **is in** the present, **but** exactly the contrary **in** retrospection. In the latter, the hours of **dull** monotony dwindle down to nothing, while those which have been characterised by a host of varied impressions grow and increase in the same degree. . . In this measurement of time **the** intervals of unimportant tranquillity go for nothing, and two important moments, even if separated by years, link themselves inevitably together. Thus, when before going to sleep we have been actively engaged on any matter, on awaking in the morning we often take up the same chain of thought, and all the intervening dreams vanish into their unsubstantial obscurity. So it is with dramatic exhibitions; our imagination passes with ease over those periods in which nothing important takes place, and dwells solely on those decisive moments placed before it, and by the concentration of which the poet gives wings to the slow course of hours and of days."(21)

And so also Dr Johnson—

"A lapse of time is as easily conceived as a passage of hours. In contemplation, we easily contract the time of real actions, and therefore willingly permit it to be contracted, when we only see their imitation."

Surely this is evident. If we find no difficulty in transporting ourselves in imagination from this present day to that on which the action is supposed to happen, it is clearly just as easy to transport ourselves from that day to the following, or any succeeding one. In reading history, we easily follow the events of a whole reign, or it may be of a whole century, without moving from our armchair. The illusion produced by dramatic exhibitions is not different from that produced by **history**, poetry, or fiction. **It** may **be** intenser, inasmuch as we see the sufferings and emotions of the characters reproduced **by** real actors; but it is **not** different, except perhaps in degree. It requires no argument to show this. Were the audience to take what **they** see produced upon the stage for real events, **they** would also look upon the actors representing the characters as the characters themselves. In that case, a spectator leaving the theatre, and meeting the actor who had played the part of Brutus, would have to ask him what his feelings were when he saw Cæsar fall, **and what** his opinion was **of** his friend **Cicero's** " **Tusculan** Disputations ; " **whether he** had supped lately with Lucullus, and **whether the** Lucrine oysters and the red mullet were good, and the jar of old Falernian mellow. If, then, the illusion produced by a stage play be not different in character to that produced by history, poetry, or fiction, why should the composer of the former be bound by severer **rules** than the composer **of the** latter ? Take fiction, for instance, and let **us try** to imagine the unity **of** time applied to **that** branch of literature. Each novel would have **to** commence at **10** o'clock on the morning **of the day** preceding the wedding, and the hero would **have** to address the heroine in some such terms as these :—(Looking at his watch), " In twenty-four hours, dearest, we shall

be one. I may then now proceed to give you an
account of my life, and of all the obstacles which
have been placed in the way of our union. This
will make the hours flow swiftly by until dinner-
time. In the evening you shall give me the history
of your previous flirtations, together with an account
of all letters, locks of hair, and dried flowers preserved by you, and which you will deliver up to me.
This pleasing retrospect will probably occupy several
hours, and bring us far into the night. We can
then retire to our respective couches with the proud
consciousness of having fully accounted for the
twenty-four hours, and thus complied with · the
unity of time."

Or, let us go one step further, and try to realise
the rule applied to everyday life. A friend, relating
the history of some mutual acquaintance, says, " In
the year so and so, he was head of his school ; ten
years afterwards he fell in love, and married."
" Stop ! stop !" you would have to answer, " you
are infringing the unity of time. You must allow
ten years to elapse before you tell me about his
marriage."

But, it is said, the observance of the unities tends
to neatness of construction. By this is probably
meant that the observance of the rule compels the
dramatist to display his story in a short, concise,
and easily intelligible manner. This is so to some

extent, but we contend that **it is** at the expense **of** other beauties, **which** are of much more importance to the spectators. **It is** evident that there are very few stories which **will** lend themselves to a compression into twenty-four hours. **If the rule is** really observed, the play can only deal with **a very** small portion of the life of the characters. But as the events of that single day have nearly always been brought about by something which has occurred before, and which the dramatist is not allowed to bring upon the stage, he must then have recourse to wearisome messengers or confidants, who relate long and tedious narratives. **In other words, he** is compelled **to put before the** audience, **by** way **of** narration, **a** great **part of the events which** ought to pass before their eyes on the stage. **It** is evident that under the unity of time there can be no unwinding of a complicated plot, and no development of character ; no course of true—or any other love— depicted as running smooth, or otherwise. That **a** rigid observance of the rule of time heightens **the** effect upon the spectator is also to **be doubted.** The chances **are** that very few **members of an** audience—even among those **who are** acquainted **with** the **doctrine of the** unities—stop to inquire whether the twenty-four **hours** have been exceeded or **not. Let us** take Schlegel's illustration of **an** enthusiastic champion **of the unities** following **a** performance "watch in hand," and instead of attending to the piece, occupying himself in counting the minutes. "The Countess," he would say —"the Countess, you know, cannot possibly get over her fit of jealousy in less than six hours. You must certainly allow eight hours between that love-scene and the next. The villain can scarcely make arrangements for the murder under twelve hours; other scenes so and so much; total, twenty-eight hours and forty minutes. The piece won't do." But it cannot be denied that these are the logical consequences of the doctrine of time. Should it again become a fixed and rigid law, the dramatist will, at last, have to work according to an authorised dramatic time-table. " Ten minutes allowed for a proposal of marriage, these being as much as is necessary for the purpose." "A quarter of an hour for the discovery of the rightful heir." "Five minutes for the scene of 'Bless you both, my children!' &c." It must be remembered, however, that the first and last incidents must never occur in the same piece, for, of course, that would be a violation of the unity.

IV.

THE UNITY OF PLACE.

IN Aristotle's " Poeticon," there is, as we have before said, no mention of the unity of place. It may, however, be attributed to Trissino, and, in its original form, confined the scene to the limits of the same building. Corneille, however, in his " Troisième Discours " (1636), pleads for an enlargement of the rule, as he had already done for that of time.

" I should wish," he says, " that that which is represented upon a stage, where there are no means of changing (the scene), should be confined to a chamber, or saloon, according to choice. But that is often so difficult, that it is absolutely necessary to find some extension for the unity of place, as for that of time. . . . I still maintain that we ought to seek to observe the unity of place as far as is possible; but as it cannot be made to fit every kind of subject, I would willingly allow that that which

happened within the boundaries of a single town
should come within the unity of place. Of course,
I should not wish the stage to represent a whole
town ; that would be somewhat too vast, but
merely two or three particular places enclosed
within its walls." (22)

He then goes on to say that he would not wish the
exact spot of the scene to be specified, but only the
name of the town where the action takes place, as
" Paris, Rome, Lyons, Constantinople." Here, then,
we have already the old complaints about the difficulty of keeping within the requirements of the
unity. Voltaire, although a strenuous upholder of
the unities, speaks also of the difficulty of complying
with that of place, and seems to accept Corneille's
theory of extension to the limits of a town.

"We have before said that the imperfect construction of our theatres—continued from our ages
of barbarism down to the present day, renders the
law of place almost impracticable. The conspirators
cannot conspire against Cæsar in his own cabinet ;
people do not talk about their most secret interests
in a public place ; the same scene cannot represent
at the same time the front of a palace and that of a
temple. The stage ought to be so arranged, as to
bring before the eye all the particular spots where
the scene is laid, without injury to the unity of place.
Here a portion of a temple ; there the vestibule of

a palace ; a public square ; streets in the background ; in short, everything that **is** necessary for presenting to the eye all that the ear ought to hear. The unity of place is the whole view which the eye can embrace without difficulty." (23)

Now, what is Voltaire's meaning here ? **At first** sight, it seems impossible to suppose that he really means to suggest that different parts of the stage should represent different parts of a town. But, read by the light of his own practice in some of his pieces, this is the conclusion to which we are irresistibly led. For instance, in " Semiramis" **the** scene represents **" a** vast peristyle, **at the end of** which is the palace **of** Semiramis. Terraced gardens rise above the palace. Right, **the** temple of the Magi ; and left, a mausoleum ornamented with obelisks." The scene is then changed to " a cabinet in the palace ; " later, to " a magnificent saloon," into which, by some means or other, the mausoleum of the first scene has managed to find its way ; **and** lastly, we have the " vestibule of a temple." **Now,** with the assistance of these stage directions, **we see** what Voltaire was pleading for. **It would** have been convenient for **him to** have all these different spots upon the stage at once, so **as to** avoid a change **of scene, and** thereby comply **with** the unity. But it must be remembered too, that all these **scenes** would have **to** be interiors. A stage, simply **edged**

round with the exteriors of various buildings would have been no use to him, as that, after all, would only amount to a representation of a public place or street. We cannot, then, avoid the conclusion that he really means what he says; and that, in his violent efforts to observe the unity, he would actually have cut up the stage into bits, each of which should represent a different scene, and all of which should be before the eyes of the spectators at once.

But where did this unity of place, which caused so much trouble to Corneille and Voltaire, come from? and how did it originate? There is, as we have said, no mention of it in Aristotle, so it cannot, like the other unities, lay claim to his authority. There can be no doubt, we think, that Trissino evolved it out of the depths of his moral consciousness, in accordance with what he conceived to be the usual practice of the Greeks. That the Greeks in their practice did usually observe the unity of place is true, but here the same arguments will apply as were used in the case of the unity of time. It may be asserted, with tolerable certainty, that their practice arose, not from any obedience to a rule, but from the mere accident of their pieces being very simply constructed. When a person is to be murdered, or sacrificed, or saved from one or the other fate, it is obvious that no change of scene is required. The scene is brought to the spot of the catastrophe, and remains there. That, however, the Greek writers had no scruple about changing their scene when they wished to do so—that, in short, they knew of no rule to prevent them doing so, there are facts enough to prove. In the " Eumenides," the scene is transferred all the way from Delphi to Athens. In the "Antigone," the scene is once changed by means of the " Encyclema," and in "Ajax," there are two changes. In none of Euripides' plays is there any change, but the above instances will be enough to show that the practice was by no means universal or compulsory. There is also another circumstance which will account for the Greek dramatists confining themselves to one scene, and that is, that had they wished to transfer it elsewhere, the construction of their stage would render it difficult for them to do so. The last row of scenery, forming the background, being built up, or what we should call " a set," and also being permanent, and the same for all plays, it was impossible to change the scene in our sense of the word. When a great theatrical effect was to be produced, as, for instance, the discovery of Orestes surrounded by the sleeping Furies, or that of Ajax among the slaughtered cattle, or later, in the same play, that of his dead body, a machine called the " Encyclema " was used. This, however, only occupied the centre portion of the stage, and was not large enough to contain any very great number of persons. It was used to represent the interior of a building, or suddenly to disclose any " tableau " which the dramatist wished to place quickly before the eyes of the audience. Beyond this, there was no machinery by which a change of scene, in our sense of the word, could be effected, and this may go far to account for the fact, noticed by Trissino, that the Greeks almost invariably confined themselves to one scene.

But if we turn again to the French dramatists, we shall find that they could no more observe the unity of place than that of time. Corneille, in his frank confessions in the " Examination " attached to each of his plays, saves us some trouble, and with extreme candour, not only acknowledges those mistakes which are apparent, but even others which we should scarcely have found out for ourselves.

"The unity of place," he says, speaking of the " Cid," " has given me no less trouble. I have placed the scene at Seville, although Don Fernando was never master of that town. I was, however, forced to this falsification in order to give some probability to the invasion of the Moors, who would be unable to get there as quickly by land as by water. I should, however, not like to assert that the tide comes up as high as that point ; * but as in the case

* It does not.

of our Seine, it has farther to go than it would have on the Guadalquivir to reach that town, that fact would suffice to give colour to the probability of its doing so, at any rate to those who have not been on the spot itself. . . . Everything, then, takes place at Seville, and thus some sort of general unity is observed; the particular spot, however, changes from scene to scene, and is, at one time, the palace of the king; at another, the apartments of the Infante; at another, the house of Chimene; and again, a street, or public place. In the detached scenes it is easy enough to determine it, but for those which have a connection with each other, it is difficult to fix upon a spot which will do for all. The Count and Don Diego get into a quarrel as they are coming out of the palace; that might take place in the street; but after receiving the box on the ear, Don Diego could not remain in the street relating his injuries, and waiting for his son to come up, without being surrounded by a crowd, and receiving offers of assistance from some of his friends. It would, therefore, be more just that he should bewail his injuries at home, where he would be able to give free course to his feelings. But in that case it would be necessary to separate the scenes, as the Spanish author has done. As they are in my piece, it may be allowable to say that the spectator must sometimes come to the assistance of the stage, and supply, in a favourable sense, those incidents which cannot be represented. Two persons stop in the street to speak with each other; it must also be presumed that from time to time they walk on; but this one cannot place before the eyes of the audience, because they might disappear from their view before being able to say that which they have to communicate to them. Let us then, by a stage fiction, imagine that Don Diego and the Count, on coming out from the palace, advance quarrelling with each other; and that they have arrived just in front of the house of the former, when he receives the box on the ear, which compels him to go in to seek assistance. If this poetical fiction should not satisfy you, then let us leave him in the public square; but in that case we must be allowed to say that the crowd around him, and the offers of service which his friends make him, are circumstances which the romance writer certainly ought not to forget; but as these subordinate incidents do nothing to assist the principal action, there is no necessity for the poet to encumber himself with them on the stage." (24)

Now, this extract is tolerably long, but Corneille's whole explanation is very much longer. The "Cid," as it stands, is a noble play (notwithstanding the box on the ear), so that all this special pleading, this petty anxiety about the unities, cause

the latter to seem somewhat small in our eyes. The
chief impression which these elaborate defences
make upon us is one of astonishment that Corneille
should ever have consented to be bound by them.
But if we turn to the " Examination " attached to
each of his other plays, we shall find that in almost
every case there is some hitch about the unities.
Thus in " Horace," "although the unity of place
is observed, it is not without some difficulty. It
is a fact that Horatius and Curatius have no
reason for separating themselves from the rest of
the family at the beginning of the second act. It
is, therefore, a piece of theatrical sleight-of-hand to
give no reasons at all when one is unable to give
good ones. The attention of the spectator to the
action going on before him will often prevent his
descending to a strict examination as to whether this
is right or wrong ; and it is no crime to take advantage of it to dazzle him, when there is a difficulty
about satisfying him." (25) In " Cinna," " there is
a doubling of the scene of action, which is quite
peculiar. One-half of the piece passes at the house
of Emilius, and the other in the cabinet of Augustus."
However, after more long explanations, it is satisfactory to find that, after all, the unity is observed,
" for the whole of the action might pass, not only
in Rome, or in a single quarter of Rome, but even in
the palace of Augustus alone, provided that you will

give Emilius an apartment there, separated from
that of Augustus." As to "Polyeucte," "the
unity of place is tolerably exact, as everything passes
in a saloon or antechamber common to the apartments of Felix and his daughter. The proprieties
would seem to be a little strained, in order to preserve the unity, in the second act, as Pauline comes
to this antechamber for the purpose of meeting
Severus, instead of waiting for his visit in her own
room." She has, however, her reasons for this, &c.
&c. "La mort de Pompée " will pass muster with
some explanations; and as regards " Rodogune,"
none at all are given with reference to the unities.
We are, then, rather surprised to find that " Heraclius"
requires the same indulgence with regard to the
unity of place as " Rodogune." And further, that
as " the majority of pieces which follow also need
it, I shall save myself the trouble of repeating this
remark in my future ' Examinations.'"

It will be seen, then, that in scarcely any single
piece of Corneille's is the unity fairly and strictly
observed. If you will imagine this, and if you will
imagine the other. If you will suppose that he or
she comes out of the house, or goes into the house,
or is in that particular place, and for that particular
reason. In some cases you may select the scene
yourself; take your choice. If the house should not
suit you, try the street; but in that case you must,

in your imagination, suppress the **traffic, the passers-
by,** and the vehicles, and fancy that a man is **stand-
ing** quite alone in a crowded thoroughfare. **If you**
will do all this, **then** we may say that everything
is in order, and that **we have** observed the unities
very cleverly !

But Voltaire's audacity, with respect to the unity
of time, is infinitely more amusing that Corneille'
timidity. The latter, at least, gives one the
impression of a man trying to do what he conceived to be his duty. Voltaire, on the contrary,
appears as a writer, who, while strenuously main-
taining certain theories, **knowingly** and wilfully
evades them, **and** trusts **to** the general stupidity of
the public **not to** be found out. **We** have already
seen that Corneille almost always allows himself
the full latitude he claims in his " Discours." He
changes the scene at will within the walls of a
town, but does not go beyond that. Now, it is
difficult to find out from Voltaire's own words what
his notion of the unity of time really was. **That he**
considers the unities to be absolutely **necessary :**
that, from their disregard of them, Shakespeare and
the English writers were mere **barbarians :** that,
through their observance of **them,** the French
dramatists (including himself) **had** entirely sur-
passed and extinguished the Greek classic writers—
all this is **clear enough** from **the various prefaces,**

dedicatory epistles, &c., attached to his plays. In one place he says that "the unity of place ought to include the whole area of a palace," but in a passage already quoted he seems to accept Corneille's theory of a whole town being available. Nor does his practice throw much more light on the subject. As far as we can judge, his fixed idea seems to be that the scene ought to be changed as rarely as possible ; for upon no other grounds can we account for the absurdities he allows himself to commit. In "Brutus," for instance, the scene is on the Tarpeian Hill. Aruns and Brutus enter, and join the characters already on the stage. The latter, it is to be presumed, retire, although there is no stage direction to that effect. The third scene takes place between Brutus and Aruns, who " are *supposed* to have quitted the hall of audience, and gone into another apartment in the house of Brutus." (26) Now, it must be remembered that Aruns and Brutus have never quitted the stage. They are still "on" when they are "supposed" to have entered another apartment. Whether the spectators are also "supposed" to take for an apartment a scene representing an open space, it is impossible to say. Look at it as we will, this stage direction defies explanation. Only one thing is evident, and that is, that Voltaire wished à *tout prix* to avoid a change of scene. Passing on to " Zaire " we find that the scene is laid, and the whole piece played from beginning to end, in the " Seraglio" **of** Jerusalem. Men of all sorts, Mohammedans, Christians, and slaves, come in and go out, as **if** the " Seraglio" were merely **a** synonym **for an open** street.　In the **third act** of " Mérope," the scene is opened **in** order to disclose the tomb of Cresphontes.　**The** tomb, however, having done its duty, has to **be** got rid of again by some means.　Now, will it be believed that Voltaire actually turns one of the characters into a scene-shifter ?　Eurycles, in leading off Egisthus, " closes the back **of** the stage behind him."　**In** " Tancrède," **we** have also a change **of** scene in **the** middle **of** the act—but no, **we** beg pardon, the " scene opens, and discloses Amenaide surrounded by guards."　But Voltaire's highest flights are reserved for " Semiramis."　The scene, as we have already said, represents an open space, surrounded by certain buildings, and with the tomb of Ninus on the left.　Everything goes on very smoothly until the middle of the third act, when the above scene " gives way to a large **saloon,** magnificently decorated." (27)　Thus, **then,** Semiramis, as we suppose, sitting in **her** chair, is transported in one instant from the **open** air into the large saloon.　But this is not **all.**　The tomb of Ninus, " ornamented with obelisks," which decorated the former scene, is positively brought with

D

Semiramis into the drawing-room; not, we must remember, a mere representation of a tomb, no model of the last resting-place of the departed, but the actual tomb itself, with its owner inside it. After this flight of genius, everything becomes indifferent to us :. there is another change of scene to "the vestibule of the temple," but we have no energy left to stop to inquire why or wherefore.

If we have not as yet mentioned Racine, it is because, on the whole, his tragedies are really much more "correct" than those of Corneille and Voltaire. Racine allows himself no extension of the unity of place in its original form. He confines himself rigorously not only to the limits of one building, but in most cases to one room. Of course this entails numerous improbabilities; but in any case, he does not run about with his scene as Voltaire does. For instance, in "Andromaque," the scene is in an apartment of the palace of Pyrrhus. In this apartment in his own palace, Orestes makes love to Pyrrhus's mistress, and announces more than once his intention of killing him, an intention which he subsequently carries out. The same thing occurs in "Britannicus." The plot against the hero is arranged in a room in his own palace. In "Bajazet," the scene, like that of "Zaire," is laid in the seraglio. Racine is quite aware of the absurdity of this arrangement, for in the opening lines of the play he attempts **to** give **an excuse for it.** In answer to a very natural question **on Osmin's** part as to how this happens, Acomat promises to explain the matter to him later, requesting him in the meantime **to "cease** these superfluous remarks." When the explanation does come, it may certainly **apply to** Acomat's presence there, but by no means accounts for the fact of Osmin being allowed to run **in** and out as he likes through five long acts. Racine, too, chose very simple subjects. Many of his plays are modelled on the old Greek drama, and founded on the same stories ; so that their simplicity **of plot** lent itself more easily **to the** observance **of the** unities. **But even with** these advantages, **he** frequently, **as we** have seen, found himself **in diffi-**culties, and often had to sanction improbabilities in order to keep within the law.

But we have come to that interpretation of the unity of place which finds such general acceptance in the present day, namely, that the scene should never be changed within the course of an act. **This** idea owes **its** origin to Corneille, who suggested **it** in his " Troisième Discours." His words **are—"** In order to rectify, **to some** extent, this **doubling of the** scene, **I** would suggest, **when it is** inevitable, that **one** should **do two** things. First, that the scene should never be changed in the same act, but only from one to **the** other, **as is the** case with the three

first acts of ' Cinna.' " (28) The second suggestion
is, that no particular spot should be given for the
scene, but only the name of the town where it takes
place, as Paris, Rome, &c. Neither of these pro-
positions was accepted in Corneille's time, or by his
followers. Voltaire, as we have seen, understood
the unity of place in quite a different sense, and in
point of fact, when he does change the scene, it is
almost always in the middle of an act. Corneille's
suggestion then seems to have found no favour for
more than a century. Nor was it, as far as we
know, alluded to by any writer on the subject, until
Marmontel's time. The latter, however, seems to
have been favourably impressed with the idea, and
in his " Elements de Littérature," strongly recommends it for adoption. His words are—

"The interval between the acts is an absence
both of actors and of spectators. The actors then
may easily be supposed to have moved from one
place to another during that interval; and the
spectators also not being tied to one place, are every-
where where the action takes place. If, then, the
action is moved from one place to another, they
move with it. But, moreover, it ought to be shown
that this displacement of the action is probable and
likely, and for this an interval is necessary. The
place, then, ought scarcely ever to be changed from
one scene to another, but only in the interval be-

tween two acts. **I am quite** aware that in order **to** facilitate a change in **the** middle of **an act, it is quite** possible to interrupt the connection of the scenes, and to leave the stage **for** a moment empty ; but this **is** not long enough to maintain the **sense of** reality, **especially** if the same actors we have just seen appear at once on the new scene **of** action. After all, it is by no means putting too great a constraint upon dramatists to exact from them a rigorous unity of place for each act, together with the moral possibility of a change from one place to another in the supposed interval." **(29)**

How, however, **this** interpretation **came to be** received **in the** present **day** was, in all probability, through Sir Walter Scott's **article on** the " Drama " in the *Encyclopædia Britannica.* He strongly re-commends the continuity of scene for each act, and, to all appearance, adopted the idea from the above passage in Marmontel. That the rule in this sense was never adopted, **or** acted upon, until quite recent times, it will **be** very easy to show. **As we** have said, Voltaire's changes of scene **are** almost always in the course of an act. In **the** only two English tragedies **ever** avowedly **written** in accord-ance with the unities, viz., Congreve's " Mourning Bride," and Addison's **" Cato,"** the same thing occurs. In the former the scene **is** changed in the second **act** from " an aisle of a temple" to " a place of

tombs;" and again in the fifth act, from "a room
of state" to "a prison." In "Cato," the scene is
changed, in the fourth act, from "a garden" to "before
the palace." We see, then, that while the unity of
time has remained unaltered, that of place has been
subject to considerable modifications. As originally
understood by Trissino, it confined the scene to one
building. By Corneille and Voltaire this limitation
was extended to the whole area of a town; and at
the present day it seems to be understood as for-
bidding a change of scene within the limits of an
act. Now all these different forms of the rule can
only have as their foundation the same theory as
the unity of time, namely, that the imagination is
incapable of following a rapid transition from one
place to another. But, as in the case of unity of
time, we ask, Is this so? If the spectator can in a
moment transport himself from his seat in the boxes
to the place where the action is laid, surely he is
able to transfer his imagination, just as easily and
rapidly, from that place to another one. To suppose
him unable to do so is only another form of con-
tending that the illusion of the stage is a real one,
and the fallacy of this we endeavoured to show in
treating of the unity of time. Dr Johnson, in his
" Preface to Shakespeare," has some remarks which,
we think, effectually dispose of that point.

"The objection," he says, "arising from the

impossibility of passing **the** first hour at Alexandria and the next at Rome, supposes that, when
the play opens, the spectator really imagines himself at Alexandria, and believes that his walk to the
theatre has been **a** voyage to Egypt, and that he lives
in the days **of** Antony and Cleopatra. Surely **he**
that imagines this may imagine more. He that
can take the stage at one time for the palace of the
Ptolemies, may take it, in half an hour, for the pro-
montory of Actium. Delusion—if delusion be ad-
mitted—has no certain limitation. If the spectator
can be persuaded that his **old** acquaintances **are**
Alexander and Cæsar; that **a** room illuminated **with**
candles **is the plain** of **Pharsalia, or** the banks of
the Granicus, **he is** in **a state of** elevation above the
reach of reason or of truth, and from the heights of
empyrean poetry may despise the circumscriptions
of terrestrial nature. . . . It is therefore evident that
the action is not supposed to be real; and it follows
that no more account of space or duration is **to be**
taken by the auditor of a drama, than by **the reader**
of a narrative, before whom may pass in **an** hour
the life of a hero or the revolutions of an empire."

   But, it will be said, by an observance of the unity
of place neatness of construction is promoted. This
we take to mean, that, **by** limiting the change of
scene to the interval between the acts, an impression
of conciseness is produced, which increases **the effect**

on the spectators. Now, to a spectator uninstructed in the mysteries of the unities, it is a very open question whether this is so. Take the case of " The Rivals," for instance. In the third act of that witty comedy, there are no less than four different scenes ; but it is very doubtful whether a spectator who had never heard of the unities would, on that account, find his enjoyment of the piece impaired. It is, indeed, even possible to imagine a man—again guileless of the unities—who would prefer a frequent change of scene, as giving variety and bustle to the piece. Of course, an enthusiastic defender of the unities will deny this. He will say, The effect of a piece upon me is materially increased by an observance of these dramatic laws ; while his opponent will allege that to him it makes no difference one way or the other. It is assertion against assertion, and opinion against opinion, and about a matter of opinion there can be no argument.

We have seen, then, that the French writers, influenced by Trissino's example, incautiously adopted rules which led them into numerous embarrassments. Trissino's " Sophonisba," in the simplicity and treatment of its subject, was a close imitation of the Greek model. The French writers, however, found that when they came to apply these rules to more complicated subjects, they could only do so, either by straining them to their utmost limits, or by evading them altogether. We have seen **Cor**-neille pleading piteously for the correctness **of his** pieces, and even going so far **as to** give us our choice of scene. We have seen Racine and **V**oltaire caus-**ing the whole** action **of a** play **to** take place **in the** Seraglio. We have seen Voltaire "bringing the **places to the** persons," changing the scene while the characters are on the stage, causing his personages to shift the scene for themselves, and positively transporting a tomb from its resting-place outside into the drawing-room. **Are we** to suppose, then, that should these rules be re-imposed here, the same results will **not** follow? Should the dramatist **be** not allowed to **take** his audience **to the** crossing-**sweeper's** cottage, he will most certainly bring **the** crossing-sweeper into the palace ; and thereby, as Lessing says, cause the improbability of the observ-ance **of** the rules to be greater than if they were not observed at **all.** These are all considerations to which the advocates **of** the unities should direct their careful attention. They must remember that the weight of proving their **case** lies **with them.** The question of the unities has, **in** England, always been more or less of an esoteric one. **It** cannot be said that there **is, or** has ever been, any very general knowledge or appreciation **of the** subject among the British public. Johnson is, **as far** as we know, the only English writer who has ever treated of the unities, and he disapproved of and opposed them. In the whole school of English writers there are only two instances of plays written avowedly in accordance with the unities. This disregard of those pedantic rules earned for us the mistaken contempt of Voltaire and Laharpe; but they, at the same time, gained for us the hearty admiration and imitation of such writers as Göthe, Lessing, and Schiller.

It is then for those who lead dramatic criticism in this country to consider whether it be a judicious thing to enforce rules which have, here at least, always been ignored and rejected. They must remember, too, that in order to do this effectually, they ought to be prepared to refer us to works written in accordance with the unities, which we should be willing to exchange for the plays of Shakespeare or the comedies of Sheridan.

THE UNITIES IN THE PRESENT CENTURY, AND IN ENGLAND.

FOR three hundred years, then, in Italy, and for two hundred in France, the dramatic unities reigned supreme. It was, too, strangely enough, in Italy, the country where they had had their rise, that the first movement was made to throw off their authority. As Trissino's "Sophonisba" had been the first piece written in accordance with the unities, so Manzoni's "Il Conte di Carmagnola" was the first written in defiance of and in opposition to them. This play was produced in the year 1820, and from **the** fact of its being an attempt **to** overthrow the old established theories, immediately attracted wide notice. **On these grounds, it** was mentioned favourably by **Göthe, who, in his** criticism of the piece, **says**—

"In his preface the writer farther plainly declares that **he** has torn himself **loose** from the severe ordinances of time and place. **He quotes** August

Wilhelm von Schlegel's writings on the subject as
conclusive, and points out the injurious effects of the
painfully constrained treatment of subjects, which
has obtained up to the present time. It is true,
that, so far, a German finds nothing which he did
not know before; he sees nothing which he would
wish to contradict. But, notwithstanding, Manzoni's remarks are worthy of all consideration on
our part. For, although this subject has for years
been thoroughly discussed and thoroughly disputed
in Germany, yet an intelligent man who finds
himself impelled to defend a good cause afresh, and
under other circumstances, will always discover a
new aspect of the question from which it ought to
be regarded and appraised, and will endeavour to
weaken and to combat the arguments of his opponents by adducing new considerations. So, too,
our author brings forward much which recommends
itself to common sense, and pleasurably affects even
those who are already convinced." (30)

Göthe also refers in a later notice of the work to
an article in our own *Quarterly Review*. His
chief object is to object to some of the reviewer's
opinions of the piece, but the passage is interesting
to us as giving an idea of the state of opinion in
England at that time with regard to the unities.
The reviewer says—

"The author of the ' Conte di Carmagnola,'

Alessandro Manzoni, in his preface, **boldly declares** war against the unities. **To** ourselves, 'chartered libertines,' as we consider ourselves on the **authority** of Shakespeare's example and Johnson's arguments, little confirmation **will** be gained from this **proselyte to** our tramontane notions **of** dramatic liberty; we fear, however, that the Italians will require a more splendid violation of their old-established laws,' &c. (*Quarterly Review*, December 1820.)

But let us now turn to Manzoni's preface **itself,** which also has an interest as being the first protest made by **a** dramatist against the tyranny **of the** unities.

" **In** Italy," **he** says, " these rules **have been** followed as **laws,** as far as **I** know, **without dis-** cussion, and consequently, most likely **without** examination." (31)

He then proceeds—

" Among the various expedients imagined **by** men for getting themselves reciprocally into trouble, one of the most ingenious is that of having, almost for every subject, **two** contradictory maxims, **and** each of which is equally looked upon as infallible. Applying this practice to even the unimportant interests of poetry, they **say to those who** cultivate it, ' Be original,' *and,* 'Write nothing **of** which the great poets have not left you **the** example.' These commands, which render **the** art still more **difficult**

than it was before, deprive also the writer of all
hope of being able to do justice to any poetical
undertaking. . . . The unity of place, and the so-
called unity of time, are not rules founded on a true
conception of the (dramatic) art : nor are they con-
formable to the nature of dramatic poetry. On the
contrary, they proceeded from authorities which
were not properly understood, and from principles
which were entirely arbitrary. . . . Lastly, the
rules render impossible many beauties, and produce many inconveniences."

If, however, it required nearly a century for the
unities to make their way from Italy into France, it
was not so with the opposition to them. The re-
bellious spirit soon spread into the latter country,
and gave rise to those fierce literary conflicts known
as the war of the " Classicists," and " Romanticists."
Among the foremost champions of the " romantic "
school, and who contended for liberty of composition
as opposed to the bondage of the unities, were
Madame de Stael, Victor Hugo, Alfred de Vigny,
Sainte-Beuve, Jules Janin, and Alexandre Dumas.
In the year 1827 Victor Hugo published his
" Cromwell," and in the preface to that play
violently attacked the doctrines of the unities,
" brushing them," as Janin says, "on one side like
spiders' webs." He commences with a somewhat
mysterious dissertation upon the " grotesque " in

ne drama, and coming **at length to the unities,**
thus proceeds—

" The wonderful thing **is,** that **the** followers **of**
routine profess to found their rule **of** the two unities
upon probability, whereas it is precisely reality which
kills **it.** What, for instance, more improbable, /
what more absurd than this vestibule, this peristyle,
this antechamber, this commonplace scene, where
our tragedies condescend to come to unwind
themselves; where the conspirators appear, why or
wherefore **we** are ignorant, to declaim against **the**
tyrant, the tyrant against **the** conspirators—each
in his turn, as **if they were** saying to each other in a
bucolic manner—

' Alternis cantemus : amant **alterna** Camenæ.'

The unity of time, too, is just as feeble as the unity
of place. The action, imprisoned by force within the
space of twenty-four hours, is just as ridiculous as
imprisoned in the vestibule. Every action has its own
proper duration of time, just as it has its own proper
scene. **To** serve out exactly the same dose **of time**
to all sorts of events ! To apply **the** same measure
to everything ! **How** we should laugh **at a** cobbler
who wished **to** put the same **shoes** upon all feet !
To interlace the unity **of time** with the unity of
place like the bars of a cage, **and** then in a pedantic
way to force into it by the **grace of** Aristotle all

those occurrences, all those nations, all those faces, which in real life Providence puts before us in such overpowering masses—to do this, is to mutilate men and facts, and to put history to grin through a horse-collar. Or let us rather say, nothing can survive this operation; and it is in this way that the dogmatic mutilators attain their usual results. That which was full of life in the chronicle, is dead in the tragedy; and it is thus that, in most cases, the cage of the unities contains nothing more than a skeleton.

" Again, if twenty-four hours can be compressed into two, it is only logical that four should contain forty-eight. The unity of Shakespeare will then be something different from the unity of Corneille. Pity ! Such, however, are the petifogging obstacles which, for two centuries, mediocrity, envy, and routine have placed in the way of genius. It is thus that they have curtailed the flights of our greatest poets. It is thus that, with the scissors of the unities, they have clipped their wings. And what have they given us in exchange for these eagle's plumes cut from Corneille and Racine ?—Compistron." (32)

We cannot profess to have any knowledge of Compistron or his works, but it appears from a biographical dictionary that he was a contemporary and friend of Racine's. His tragedies, which were tolerably numerous, were formed on the **model of** those of Racine, and, according **to** the biographer, "possess many beauties," an opinion with which Victor Hugo does not seem **to** agree.

Hugo continued, in various publications, to urge his views in favour of what he termed liberty and tolerance **in** composition, but it was not until the production of " Hernani " at the Théâtre Français, the 21st of February 1830, that the question may be said to have come to a final settlement. The struggle was violent, and the victory for some time doubtful; but at the conclusion of the performance there was no longer any doubt that **it** remained **on the** side **of** the " Romanticists."

" **The two** parties," says a French account, " met (*s'etaient donné rendezvous*), at the first performance **of** 'Hernani,' as on a field of battle. The 'Romanticists,' however, carried the day." In an English biography of Victor Hugo, we read that "in 1830 his ' Ernani ' was played for the first time at the Théâtre Français. The indignation of **the** old, and the enthusiasm **of** the new, party **knew no bounds.** The first performance **of** ' Ernani ' **was a scene of** riotous confusion, **and** pugilistic en-**counters** filled up the intervals **between the** acts. Meanwhile the drama, which **was far** superior in construction to ' Cromwell,' succeeded. "

This performance was **decisive as** to the fate of

E

the unities in France, and may be considered to have given them their deathblow. From that time up to the present day no dramatist has been expected to guide himself according to the law of the unities, nor has, as far as we know, any critic ventured to recommend or to uphold their maintenance in that or in any other country.

In attempting to estimate the influence of the unities on English tragedy, we meet with some little difficulty. That they were known in England towards the close of the seventeenth century, there is abundant evidence to show. Congreve's "Mourning Bride" (1697) is especially praised by Voltaire for its conformity to the unities, in contradistinction to the other "barbarous" productions of the English stage. If, however, we try to form an opinion from the writings of other dramatists of the period as to how far they were influenced by the unities, it is not always easy to come to a conclusion. It is almost needless to say that we search in vain through the works of Shakespeare, Ben Jonson, Beaumont and Fletcher, Massinger and Ford, for any traces of the unities. The first piece in English dramatic literature in which they distinctly appear is Otway's fine play "Venice Preserved" (1682). He is careful to let us know that the first act takes place in the morning or afternoon; the second act, as he tells us, just before and after midnight; and in the third act,

the events of the second one are alluded to **as having**
happened "last night." He would **then apparently**
have us suppose that the fourth **and fifth** acts occupy
the morning **and afternoon of** the second day. If
this be **so, we** must again urge the old objection,
namely, **that** although such a series of events *might*
happen in twenty-four hours, it is very unlikely that
they should. As to the unity of time, the frequent
changes of scene would be rather puzzling, did we
not know that at that time change of scene in the
course of an act did not **of** itself constitute an in-
fraction of **the unity.** Although there **are** nine **scenes**
in the whole play, **and two** changes in the second
and the fifth acts respectively, **yet the** action is not
allowed to travel beyond the **limits of one** town ; and
this was, at the time, probably looked upon as a
fulfilment of the unity. Notwithstanding, however, these numerous changes, it would appear as if
still more were required. It seems to be the height
of improbability that Belvedera should, in the
second act, be allowed to attend the meeting of **the**
conspirators ; and still more improbable that **she**
should be willing to attend it **in the place set**
down for it, namely, " Aquilina's **house, the**
Greek courtesan." **Again, in the** fourth act, it
seems very unlikely that **she** should have had the
permission to wander **at will** about the building
where the senate held their sittings, and even into

the council-chamber during a secret assemblage of the senate.

If, however, we turn to the same writer's " Orphan," produced two years earlier (1680), it is almost impossible to make out whether the author intended to conform to the unities or not. The changes of scene are not so frequent as in " Venice Preserved," and, in the second and third acts, one scene suffices all through. As to the unity of time, we think on the whole that the writer really intended the action not to extend beyond one day; but if so, in this case again the day must have been a most eventful one.

Southern's " Isabella, or The Fatal Marriage " (1694), also shows signs of the unities. The events might pass in a single day, and we think, from Villeroy's impatience to " send for the priest " at once, that the writer intended they should.

Of " The Mourning Bride " (1697), we have already said that the unities are rigidly observed. We next come to Rowe's " Tamerlane " (1702), in which no traces of the unities are to be found. In the same author's " Fair Penitent " (1703), it is difficult to say whether they exist or not. The unity of place is observed according to the modern notion of it, there being only one scene for each act. When, however, we come to look for the unity of time, it is not easy to discover the author's intention. The events **of** the first four acts might perhaps be made to pass within twenty-four hours, but whether those of the fifth act could be compressed into the latter part **of** the second day must be **a** matter **of** opinion.

In going through the list of **the best** English tragedies **of** the eighteenth century, we **find a** considerable dearth of excellence at its commencement. No piece has been found worthy of preservation, in the best collections of the time, between the years 1703 and 1713, the date of the production of "Cato." It might have been supposed that the great success of this play would have **had the** effect **of** inducing **other** writers to imitate **its** obedience to the unities. This, **however,** does not seem to have been the case. We search in vain for any traces of them in "Jane Shore" (1713), "Lady Jane Grey" (1715), "The Siege of Damascus" (1720), and "The Revenge" (1721). Fenton's "Mariamne" (1723) would seem to have been written in **accord**ance with the unities; but it is needless to say **that** our old friend "George Barnwell" **(1730) is en**tirely innocent **of** them. The same **writer's "Fatal** Curiosity" **(17**37) will fall in with them; but in **his other** play, "**Arden** of Feversham" (1739), he again ignores them. In "King Charles I." (1737), and "Gustavus Vasa" (1738), the unities are also wanting, **until** we come to Thompson's violent piece,

"Tancred and Sigismunda" (1745), where they again appear. This brings us to Dr Johnson's tragedy "Irene," produced at Drury Lane, February 1749. Now, from the opinion which, as we shall presently see, Johnson a few years later expressed with regard to the unities, we should have expected that, in his one tragedy, he would have treated them with contempt. This, however, is not the case. The piece is written throughout with a strict regard to those very unities which he, a short time afterwards, so successfully criticised, and, as far as the English stage was concerned, may be said to have utterly demolished. The date of Johnson's "Preface to Shakespeare," in which this criticism appeared, was 1756, and a reference to the following tabulated statement will show that after that date, up to the end of the century, no single tragedy can be pointed out in which the unities are strictly maintained.

Tragedies written in accordance with the unities.

Venice Preserved (Otway), 1682.
Mourning Bride (Congreve), 1697.
Cato (Addison), 1713.
Mariamne (Fenton), 1723.
Fatal Curiosity (Lillo), 1737.
Tancred and Sigismunda (Thompson), 1745.
Irene (Johnson), 1749.
Elfrida (Mason), written 1752, C. G. 1772.
Caractacus (Mason), written 1759, C. G. 1776.

Boadicea (Glover), 1753.
Barbarossa (Brown), 1755.

Tragedies in which the unities are not maintained.

Oronooko (Southern), **1696.**
Tamerlane (Rowe), 1702.
Jane Shore (Rowe), 1713.
Lady Jane Grey (Rowe), 1715.
Distressed Mother (Philips), 1712.
Siege of Damascus (Hughes), 1720.
The Revenge (Young), 1721.
The Brothers (Young), 1726.
George Barnwell (Lillo), 1730.
Arden of Feversham (Lillo), 1739.
King Charles I. (Howard), 1737.
Gustavus Vasa (Brooke), 1738.
Roman Father (Whitehead), **1750.**
Gamester (Moore), **1753.**
Earl of Essex (Jones), **1753.**
Douglas (Home), **1757.**
Cleone (Dodsley), 1759.
Earl of Warwick (Franklin), 1766.
Grecian Daughter (Murphy), 1772.
Matilda (Brown), 1775.
Countess of Salisbury (Hartson), 1767.
Percy (Hannah More), 1778.
Fair Apostate (Macdonald), 1788.
Pizarro (Sheridan), 1799.

Doubtful.

Orphan (Otway), **1680.**
Isabella (Southern), 1694.
Fair Penitent (Rowe), **1703.**

It will be seen, then, that although after the
publication of Johnson's " Preface to Shakespeare,"

in 1756, the unities were tacitly allowed to disappear, yet that between the years 1680 and 1756 they exercised a very undoubted influence on the English stage.   The fact seems to have been that many writers, while in reality half disapproving of them, still felt them too strong to be altogether ignored. Of this we have a curious instance in the cases of Addison's "Cato" and Johnson's "Irene." In Addison's papers in the *Spectator* on the improvement of the stage (Nos. 39, 40, 42, and 44), he does not venture to recommend the observance of the unities. Now it must be remarked that, at the very time he was writing them (they appeared in April 1711), he must have been engaged in preparing "Cato" for the stage.   In fact, he was actually accused by Dennis of writing these papers in order to influence the public mind for the reception of his piece.   In these papers there are a great many useful hints, and a great deal of common sense, but not a word of the unities.   Surely, if he had had such a high opinion of them as we might suppose from his piece, he would have taken this opportunity of defending them, and recommending them for universal adoption. The case of Johnson is quite as singular.   His tragedy is produced in 1749, and strictly follows the dictates of the unities; but seven years later we find him arguing that the unities are by no means essential, but that they are, on the contrary, an obstacle to many kinds of excellence. **We have already** quoted part of this criticism on the subjects **of time** and place, but the reader would do well to refer to its entirety, **as an** example of vigorous reasoning, **and** as making out **an** almost overwhelming case against the unities. The conclusion at which he arrives **is as** follows :—

" The result of my inquiries is that the unities of time and place are not essential to a just drama ; that though they may sometimes conduce to pleasure, they are always to be sacrificed to the nobler beauties of variety and instruction ; and that **a** play written with nice observation of the critical **rules is to** be contemplated as an elaborate curiosity, as the product **of** superfluous and ostentatious art, **by** which **is** shown rather what is possible than what is necessary."—(Preface to Shakespeare.)

This criticism was the deathblow to the unities in England. From that time they disappear and leave no trace behind—unless, indeed, they are to be revived for the benefit of playgoers in **the** nineteenth century. Even, however, before **the** appearance of Johnson's crushing arguments, they seem to have been regarded, **as far** as we can judge from the literature of the **time,** with a feeling of slightly contemptuous ridicule. Pope, who furnished the prologue to "Cato," had, two years

before, in his " Essay on Criticism," thus spoken of
them—

> " Once on a time, La Mancha's knight, they say,
> A certain bard encountering on the way,
> Discoursed in terms as just, with looks as sage,
> As e'er could Dennis of the Grecian stage,
> Concluding all were desperate sots and fools
> Who durst depart from Aristotle's rules.
> Our author, happy in a judge so nice,
> Produced his play, and begged the knight's advice ;
> Made him observe the subject and the plot,
> The manners, passions, unities ; what not ?
> All which exact to rule were brought about,
> Were but a combat in the lists left out."

Altogether, as far as we can see, the doctrine of
the unities never seems to have gained the public
favour in England.

> " Bold is the man who, in this nicer age,
> Presumes to tread the chaste, corrected stage,"

says Thompson in the prologue to " Tancred and
Sigismunda ; " and Goldsmith's opinion will be
found in the following passages from the " Good-
Natured Man : "—

" *Honeywood.*—We should not be severe against
dull writers, madam. It is ten to one but the
dullest writer exceeds the most rigid French critic
who presumes to despise him.

" *Miss Rich.*—Yet, Mr Honeywood, this does not
convince me but that severity in criticism is neces-

sary. It was our first adopting the severity of the French taste that has brought them in turn to taste us.

"*Honey.*— . . . **They draw a** parallel, madam, between the mental taste and that of our **senses. We are** injured as much by the French severity in **the one** as by French rapacity in the other."

It must, however, be by no means forgotten that no attempt was ever made in this country to apply the theory of the unities to comedy. There is no English comedy, as far as we are aware, of that age, written with the determined purpose of complying with the unities. "She **Stoops** to Conquer" might, **at first** sight, seem to come under this head, **but we** think that **the** passage quoted above is enough to show that it was merely the accident of the subject which gives it this appearance. Besides, it is very improbable that Dr Johnson, after his deliberately expressed opinion as regards the unities, would have allowed his friend "Goldy" to attempt the innovation of applying them **to** comedy.

There exist **then, in** the English language, **some** dozen tragedies which show more or less obedience **to** the rules of **the** unities. **It must**, however, be observed that in most of these the unity of place is treated in a manner which we suppose in these days would be looked upon as extremely defective.

The changes of scene during the course of an act
are very frequent, and the writers evidently considered, that as long as they kept to Corneille's rule of
confining themselves within the walls of a town, they
could change about inside that town as much and
as frequently as they liked.   That this also was a
defect—if it be a defect—of the old comedies, it is
scarcely necessary to state here.   Change of scene,
whenever the purposes or even the caprices of the
writer led him to suppose it necessary, was from the
earliest times the undoubted and undisputed privi-
lege of the English dramatist.   It is possible that
in these days we are going to improve all that ; and
no one, we suppose, would object to the improvement
if there were any probability that we could by these
means again raise our stage to the level of former
days.   On reading over these old plays, it is melan-
choly to see what a noble inheritance has been
bequeathed to us, and how sadly we have disgraced
it.   For two hundred years the English stage was
as much above the French as the French, in the
present day, is above our own.   Such was once our
position, and now—we all know what we have
come to.   But, it is said, the French stage owes its
excellence to the extreme liberty accorded to its
writers in their choice of subjects.   By no means.
The French stage is great in spite of its immorality,
and not on account of it.   Look at the extraordi-

nary skill in construction displayed by their writers;
look at the freshness of their plots, and the originality of the incidents which tend to its development;
look at those wonderful little surprises, which, **like**
an "avoidance" in music, excite the interest of the
spectators in the highest degree, only agreeably **to**
disappoint them.   All these are excellences quite
independent of the violation of social laws or the
sanctity of the marriage tie.   There are quantities
of admirable French pieces written with an extreme
purity which would satisfy the most rigid prude.
Take for instance, "Mademoiselle de la Seiglière,"
"**Un** Veue d'Eau," "Bataille de Dames," **or** "Le
Roman d'un Jeune Homme Pauvre." Take them as
specimens of constructive art, or **as** pictures of
manners, and then say what have we to show against
them.   But patience !   Already there are signs of
better things.   In those rare cases, within the last
few years, where pieces written with some slight
regard for nature and for common sense have been
produced, they have been eagerly welcomed.   **There**
is no reason to doubt, then, that the public **will**
again, whenever it may get the opportunity, prefer
such pieces to **the** wild nonsense which **is** usually
set before it.

It is almost needless to say that on the dramatic
literature of the present century the unities have,
up to our day, exercised **an** all but **imperceptible**

influence.   In fact, the century may be said to commence with plays than which nothing could be
more opposed to the spirit of the unities, namely,
the strange productions of the younger Colman.
We may remark *en passant* that nothing could
exceed the poverty of the English stage between
the years 1800 and 1830.   At first this may have
been owing to the long and severe war in which the
country was engaged, but it is difficult to see why,
after the peace of 1815, the stage should have had
any difficulty in recovering itself. With the exception
of "John Bull" (1803), and "Paul Pry" (1825),
there are scarcely any pieces of this period which are
known even to the student of plays.   Judging from
the titles of the pieces produced at this time, melo-
drama of the ferocious type of the "Castle Spectre"
was in the ascendant, while, a little later, begin to
appear those adaptations of novels and of foreign
plays (principally operas) from the effects of which
we are still suffering.   As to the unities, they had
very little chance in such company, and even when
we arrive at a rather better state of things, their influence is still all but invisible.   We find no traces
of them in "Bubbles of the Day," "Retired from
Business," "The Housekeeper," or in any of Douglas
Jerrold's pieces.   In the "Duchess de la Vallière,"
"Lady of Lyons," and "Money," they are equally
wanting.   The five acts of "Richelieu" are, we are

told, divided into four days, but this will scarcely bring us nearer to the unities. " Not **so bad as we** seem," observes the unity of time, but violates **that** of place. **In Mr** Tom Taylor's best pieces there is no question **of the** unities. " Plot and Passion," " Two **Loves** and a Life," " Masks and Faces," and a " Lesson for Life," are all equally regardless of them. That admirable play, " Still Waters run Deep," observes the unity of time almost to the minute; but this may possibly arise more from the accident of the subject than from any preconceived design. We are the more inclined **to** this opinion from the fact that the unity **of** place is a little strained in the change of scene in the second **act,** and **where** sufficient time is scarcely allowed to Mildmay to appear **on** the new scene after leaving the previous one. This, however, is hypercriticism worthy of a champion of the unities, and, on the whole, we are thankful to say, Mr Tom Taylor has throughout his plays **rated** the unities at their proper worth. In Mr Dion Boucicault's plays, and in the late **Mr** Robertson's comedies, the unities are also entirely disregarded. We now, however, come to **the only** play, as far as our knowledge **goes, of the** present century, written avowedly in accordance with the unities. This is Mr Gilbert's graceful piece, " The Wicked World." Although described in the play-bill as a " fairy comedy," the same authority assures

us that the action is comprised within the space of
twenty-four hours.   As there is only one scene,
this is equivalent to saying that all the unities are
strictly followed. But as regards time, is this so ?
For a young lady to be in the morning speculating on
the nature of love, to be in the afternoon a prey
to a violent passion, and in the evening to hate the
object of that passion as intensely as she before
loved him—is surely causing events to move with
a somewhat unnatural rapidity. Not that Mr
Gilbert is singular in this. The same objection may,
as we have tried to show, be urged against ninety-
nine out of every hundred plays which attempt to
observe the unities. " The Wicked World," moreover, requires no assistance from the unities. It is
a good piece, original in conception, and graceful in
execution, and we are quite sure that no spectator
will ever interrupt his enjoyment of it to inquire
whether the unities are maintained in it or not.

We have thus endeavoured to trace the history of
the unities, from the time they were first elaborated
by Trissino out of the maxims of Aristotle, down to
the present day. Any one who carefully studies
the pieces in which they are followed can, we
think, scarcely avoid coming to the conclusion that
they are useless in themselves, a hindrance to the
dramatist, and an encumbrance on the effect and
the natural development of a play. They throw

a **dull** and frigid tone over everything they touch, and leave room for nothing but mere declamation, to the exclusion of the higher beauties of dramatic composition. Good verses **are** possible under their sway, but, beyond **this,** nothing. Action, variety of interest **or of** incident, development of story **or of character,** are alike impossible. In no plays are these defects more conspicuous than in the only two English plays which we know for a certainty to have been written in accordance with them, namely, "The Mourning Bride " and " Cato." Excellence of composition, stirring and vigorous verses, **are present** in both **of** them, but the whole **effect is** dull, cold, and depressing. The same **remark** applies to the greater number of French tragedies. They are often pedantic, bombastic, and, in some cases, silly; until our only wonder is that some of them, weighed down, as they were, by the unities, should be so good as we still find them to be. Nor can the defenders of the unities bring forward such a weight of authority as can be shown on **the** other side. On the one hand, we have Corneille, Racine, Voltaire, and Alfieri, against Shakespeare, Lopez di Vega, Calderon, Göthe, Lessing, Schiller, Manzoni, and Victor Hugo. Nor, **as** regards criticism, are they in a better position. Dr Johnson, Lessing, Schlegel, Göthe, Victor Hugo, and Jules Janin, may safely be matched against Corneille,

F

Voltaire, Laharpe, and Dennis. We would, then, try to induce our critics to pause before they endeavour to resuscitate the unities from that oblivion to which they were forty years ago consigned. They must remember that, even in France and Italy, where for two hundred years they reigned supreme, they have, since the year 1830, been utterly repudiated. In Spain they never were known, or, if known, disregarded. In Germany, after careful and minute examination on the part of such men as Lessing and Göthe, they were entirely rejected. In England, except in one or two instances, they were never acknowledged, and it may be said that the great bulk of the English public has at all times treated them with marked disdain. We quite admit that it is only natural that gentlemen of classical training and scholarly attainments should have a sort of weakness for the unities of their youth; but the question is, whether it be judicious to wish to apply to the light comedy of a day rules suitable only to tragedies formed on the classical model. A lover of Horace is delighted when he hears a correct or appropriate quotation from his favourite poet; but he ought not, on that account, to insist upon all poetry being written after the manner of Horace. But, it may be answered, although our opinions are in favour of the unities, you are not bound to follow them. But this is not so. From the moment that a dramatist finds the observance of the unities praised as a merit by his critics, he will certainly endeavour to model his plays after them, **to the** detriment, probably, of his subject, and certainly **to the** detriment of his audience. **At** the best, he will attempt **to confine** himself only to such subjects as will fit **in with the** unities, to the exclusion of others equally, and perhaps more, worthy **of** dramatic treatment. We appeal, then, we repeat, to those who lead dramatic criticism in the present day. The future is in their **hands.** Should they continue **to** recommend the maintenance of the unities, they **will be** maintained ; but **it is a** question for their consideration whether t be judicious, and for the interests of the drama, to **impose** this extra burden on a stage which is already in **by no** means a satisfactory condition.

ADDENDA.

I.

THE following facts in support of the writer's argument have been brought to his notice through the kindness of valued correspondents and friends.

In treating of the unity of time, sufficient stress has scarcely been laid on the frequent and remarkable violations of it on the part of the Greek dramatists. The more these are considered, the more, apparently, do they point to the fact that the rule of the unity of time, as laid down by Aristotle, was unknown to those writers. Either they recognised no such canon or precept, or, if they did recognise it, they reserved to themselves the right to ignore it whenever the exigencies of their pieces seemed to make it necessary or advisable. The single instance in the "Agamemnon" of Æschylus, even if it stood alone, would be almost sufficient to prove this. In the opening scene, we have the watchman posted on the roof, intently looking out for the beacon-fire which is to announce to him the fall of Troy. Presently the flame appears, and he proceeds to announce the joyful news to his mistress, Clytemnestra. The latter, in a subsequent dialogue with the chorus, explains the arrangement of the beacon-fires which were to convey her the news, and tells them that "this very day Troy is in the possession of the Greeks." After a chorus, a herald is introduced, who confirms the account of the fall of Troy, having travelled from thence since the event; and subsequently Agamemnon

E *

appears, who has also performed that journey. Now, the distance from Troy to Argos must, roughly speaking, have been some two hundred miles, and it is evident that such a journey in those times must have required many days for its accomplishment. That then the Greek dramatists were, as Schlegel says, quite above such petty anxieties of minute calculation as the strict observance of the unity of time would entail upon them, seems to be certain ; and there can be no doubt that, in endeavouring to discover how far they considered themselves bound by the rule, we may put the widest and most liberal interpretation upon the "ὅτι μάλιστα" of Aristotle.

This view is shared by Dr Müller Strübing, a learned writer, whose perfect knowledge of the Greek stage renders his authority of considerable weight. In discussing the question whether a change of scene takes place in the "Acharnians" of Aristophanes, he says—

33. "But that effect which the writers of all ages have produced by means of a change of scene—in other words, by the suspension of the continuity of place—was, to a certain extent, obtained on the Greek stage by the interruption of the dramatic action. By this means, too, they break off at the same moment—so far as the spectator is concerned—the continuity of time, and thereby gain what is an absolute necessity for the drama—an illimitable ideal course of time, instead of a fixed and limited period measurable by the exercise of the reason. And here I am reminded of the wonderful art with which Æschylus in his 'Agamemnon' has suspended the flow of time, and rendered all calculation on that point impossible. But it is in the works of the greatest master of dramatic art—of that poet who, above all others, possessed the deepest sense of—I might almost say, an innate sense for—stage effect, namely, Shakespeare, that one will find hundreds of instances where, after a change of scene, the next scene is connected in the most direct manner with the preceding one, and where yet something takes

place which infers the passage of a considerable **lapse of**
time during the change." (Müller Strübing, "Aristophanes.")
In another passage, the author warns us against imputing
to the early Attic writers a "too childish conduct as regards
time and place;" and the object of his argument is to prove
that which **we have been** endeavouring to show, namely,
that the **Greek** dramatists, whenever it was convenient to
them, **had** no scruples about changing their time and place;
and that Trissino, when he elaborated his celebrated rules,
either overlooked or ignored the numerous instances in
which they had done so.

II.

In arranging the list of those English tragedies which
were written in accordance with the unities, it entirely
escaped the writer's memory **that Lord** Byron's tragedy **of**
"Sardanapalus" came **under that** head, **and** ought to have
been included in the catalogue. **The** writer can scarcely
blame himself enough for this serious oversight, and is
especially grateful to the correspondent whose kindness
prompted him to point it out, and enabled him to refer to
it here. As Lord Byron himself tells us, he attempted in
"Sardanapalus" "to observe," and in "The Two Foscari"
"to approach, the unities; conceiving that with any very
distant departure from them, there may be poetry, but can
be no drama. He is aware of the unpopularity of this
notion in present English literature; but it is not a system
of his own, but merely **an** opinion, which, not very long **ago,**
was the law of literature throughout the world, and is still so
in the more civilised parts of it." Now, to any **one who** has
endeavoured to appraise the influence of the unities on
dramatic literature, it will occur that Lord Byron's estimate
of them is altogether an exaggerated one. When he says
that without them "there may be poetry, but can be no
drama," it will appear to many that the sentence would be
more accurate were it reversed. Had he said, "under the

unities there may be poetry, but can be no drama," the opinion would, we think, have been nearer the truth, and the critics of the "romantic" school would have been obliged to him for putting their case in so neat a form. It is evident that the unities can have no influence one way or the other upon the versification of a play ; they can neither inspire good verses, nor impede them. But it is also as evident that there might be cases in which their influence would by no means contribute to the production of a "good drama." To wish to contract all subjects into the same space of twenty-four hours, or to the limits of a single dwelling or town,—to try, as Victor Hugo says, "to fit all feet with the same shoes,"—was certainly not a very efficacious means of ensuring complicated interest of story, ingenious development of plot, multiplication of modifying incidents, or any of those other elements which serve to make a good play influence the emotions of the spectators. As to the unities "being, not very long ago, the law of literature throughout the world," to what extent this was the case, and especially in England, we have already endeavoured to show. What, however, Lord Byron meant by the words, "and is still so in the more civilised parts of it," we are quite at a loss to conceive. What particular country, in the year 1821, was in the favoured position of being more civilised than England, it would be difficult to say. Politically, England stood, at that period, at the head of Europe ; and as regards her place in literature, the following opinion was expressed by Göthe a very few years later (December 1824) in his "Conversations with Eckermann."

34. "It is of importance," said Göthe, "that you bring together a capital which will never fail you. This you will attain in that study of the English language and literature which you have already commenced. Persevere in it, and take advantage, every hour of the day, if possible, of the opportunities afforded by the presence here of the young Englishmen. The ancient languages have, for the most

part, escaped you in your youth ; therefore seek a support
in the literature of that able nation—the English. Our
own literature, moreover, **has** sprung chiefly from theirs.
Where do our tragedies and our novels come from, but from
Shakespeare, Fielding, and Goldsmith? And where can
you find in Germany, **at** the present time, three literary
heroes **to set by the** side **of** Lord Byron, Moore, and Walter
Scott? Once again, then, make yourself strong in English ;
nerve your powers to something good, and avoid everything
which can do you no credit, or which is unworthy of you."
Other passages might be quoted to show that Göthe—of all
men then living, perhaps the one best qualified to judge—
placed our literature, even of that day, at the head of all
others. It is possible, however, that what was passing
through Lord Byron's mind was some reminiscence of **certain** passages **in** Voltaire's writings, and some **of** which we
have already quoted. **It** will **be** remembered that in these
passages **the** civilisation **or** barbarism **of** a nation depends
upon its acceptance or rejection of **the** unities. Those
nations which have submitted to the yoke of the unities are
great, enlightened, and glorious ; while those which have
ignored or refused it, are dull, ignorant, and barbarous.
According to this view, then, the most civilised nations
could, at that time, only have been Italy and France. But,
as we have seen, Manzoni had already attempted to break
through his bonds, in Italy ; while, in France, that reaction
was already setting in which was to culminate in the victory
of Victor Hugo and the " Romanticists."

The passage in which Lord Byron says that he has **in one**
tragedy attempted to " approach " the unities, refers, as we
have already said, to " The Two Foscari," which was published, together **with** " Sardanapalus," in December 1821.
It is somewhat difficult to discover what Lord Byron meant
by the word " approach." Granted the falsification of
history which makes both father and son die on the same
day, the tragedy unfolds itself with all possible obedience

and submission to the unities. It was, perhaps, to this that Lord Byron referred, although the slight perversion of the real facts in the interest of the tragedy would seem to be fairly allowable. Jacopo Foscari was put to the torture, and condemned to exile, by the Council of Ten, in the year 1445. Having, in spite of his sentence, returned to Venice in the month of July 1456, he was again imprisoned, and died in the month of August or September in the same year. Francisco Foscari was summoned to resign the office of Doge, which he had held for 34 years, in October 1457. Having refused to do so, he was, as is correctly brought forward in the tragedy, dismissed, and three days afterwards died of a broken heart. Supposing the liberty taken with the story to be the only violation of the unities, most critics will probably be of opinion that the fault or blemish was by no means an unpardonable one. Anything that Jeffrey wrote with regard to Lord Byron's productions, must be received with a certain degree of suspicion; for his bias against, or personal dislike to, this author, is always more or less evident. There is, however, a certain degree of truth in his remarks about "The Two Foscari," which compel us, rather against our will, we confess, to agree with him. He says—

"The disadvantage, and, in truth, absurdity, of sacrificing higher objects to a formal adherence to the unities, is strikingly displayed in this drama. The whole interest here turns upon the younger Foscari having returned from banishment, in defiance of the law and its consequences, from an unconquerable longing after his own country. Now, the only way to have made this sentiment palatable, the practicable foundation of stupendous sufferings, would have been to have presented him to the audience, wearing out his heart in exile, and forming his resolution to return, at a distance from his country, or hovering, in excruciating suspense, within sight of its borders. We might then have caught some glimpse of his motives, and of so extraordinary a

character. But as this would have been contrary to one of
the unities, we first meet with him led from the 'Question,'
and afterwards taken back to it in the ducal palace, or cling-
ing to the dungeon-walls **of** his native city, and expiring
from his dread **of** leaving them ; and therefore feel more
wonder than sympathy when we **are** told that these agonis-
ing consequences have resulted, not from guilt **or** disaster,
but merely from the intensity of his love for his country."—
Edinburgh Review, February 1822.

But to return to "Sardanapalus." The unities were, in
this piece, the object of Lord Byron's especial attention and
care, as may be seen from his letters to Mr Murray. "I
have," he says in one place, "strictly preserved all the
unities hitherto, and mean to continue them **in** the fifth, **if**
possible." Again, "You will remark that all the unities
are strictly preserved **;" and, when the drama** was completed, "Print away, and publish." **He** writes, "Mind **the**
unities, which are **my great** object **of research."** Now, it
will **be** remembered, "Sardanapalus" is dedicated **to**
Göthe. Could Byron, **in** inscribing to Göthe a work
written with the strictest regard to the unities, have had
any special motive? He must have known that Göthe
was either ignorant of the unities, which was scarcely to be
supposed, or had deliberately rejected them. His "Faust"
alone would be enough to show that. Then why did Byron
deliberately select, as the vehicle for a compliment to Göthe,
a production, the chief glory of which was, in his own **eyes,**
its adherence to a set of rules of which he knew Göthe to
disapprove? Did **he** suppose that **he** might **possibly con-**
vert Göthe to his **own** way of thinking? **or did** he, with **a**
touch **of vanity,** wish to show him what could **be** done even
while observing the unities? **Of course there** is the other
alternative that Lord Byron, with characteristic carelessness,
thought nothing at all about the matter. He wished to pay
a compliment to Göthe by dedicating one of his works to
him, and **he** took that one which came to hand first, or,

more probably, the first one he completed after forming his resolution. This may be so; but the curious fact remains that here was a book, intended as a glorification of the unities, inscribed to one of their greatest and most resolute opponents. That Göthe was gratified by the compliment, we may very easily believe; and, in fact, an extract from some work of Göthe's, prefixed to Moore's edition of the tragedy, tells us as much. The original of the extract we have not been able to find, but it is, no doubt, authentic; and the fact is certain that Göthe had the highest admiration for Lord Byron's genius, as many passages in "Eckermann's Conversations" will show. That, however, the fact of the tragedy adhering to the unities, failed to cause him any gratification—rather the contrary, if anything, a somewhat strong passage from Eckermann will be quite sufficient to prove.

35. "Göthe said I was right, and then began to laugh about Lord Byron; a man, he said, who never having subjected himself to anything, had, at last, submitted to the silliest of all laws—those of the three unities. He understood, said Göthe, no more about the foundation of those laws than all the rest of the world. The intelligible is the proper foundation, and the three unities are only of use as far as they enable one to attain it. Given, however, that they obstruct the intelligible, it is foolish to look upon them, and to obey them, as laws. Even the Greeks, from whom they sprung, did not always observe them. In the 'Phæthon' of Euripides, as also in other pieces, the scene of action is changed; and we see from this that the due representation of their subject was of more importance to them than a blind respect for a law which of itself was of no great consequence. Shakespeare's pieces go beyond the unities of time and place as far as it is possible for them to go, but they are intelligible, nothing more so; and for that reason, even the Greeks would have held them to be irreproachable. The French poets are the strictest of all in

their endeavours to obey the law of the unities, but they
sin against the intelligible, inasmuch as they solve a dramatic
law, not in a dramatic manner, but by way of narration."

If then, as Göthe **says,** the principal object of the dramatist ought **to** be to put his story before the audience in a
clear and intelligible **manner, it** would appear that he ought
to be **the best** judge **as** to how this object is **to** be effected.
Should **he fail in** it, he lays himself open to criticism and to
blame, but the means ought to be left to his own discretion.
All restrictions which apply the same inflexible rule to all
subjects, can only, in most cases, seriously impede the production of satisfactory dramas. There are stories, of course,
which will bear compression into the space of twenty-four,
or even two, hours, and which could find no difficulty **in**
developing themselves within the limits **of a** single building,
or even of a single room. **But,** in contradistinction to these,
it is evident that the majority of plots will refuse to be bound
by such **restricted** limits. If this be **so, it** is **then** clear that
Marmontel's theory **of one scene** for each act, and which
appears to **be** widely accepted in the present **day,** rests **on** no
better theoretical foundation than the older forms of the unity
of place. Many stories will lend themselves easily enough to
this restriction, but many again can only be brought within
it by causing events to happen on a certain scene which
ought to happen elsewhere, and by bringing certain of the
characters into places where their presence is improbable and
unnatural. The connection of the unity of place with that of
time is very evident. When the action of a piece was restricted
to twenty-four hours, it was easy enough, in most cases, to
make it happen within the four walls of some certain building. On the other hand, by restricting **the unity of** place,
you restrict that of time. By confining the dramatist to a
certain number of scenes, you in all probability compel him
to leave unrepresented, a portion of that which he would
wish to place before his audience. Supposing, however,
that he should **insist** upon including these events in his

Theilnahme den Ereigniſſen zu folgen, wie ein Gefangenwärter die Uhr oder das Stundenglas in der Hand, den Helden des Trauerspiels die Stunden zuzählte, die ſie noch zu handeln und zu leben haben! ... So pflegen wir, wenn wir vor dem Einſchlafen lebhaft mit irgend etwas beſchäftigt waren, bei'm Erwachen dieſelbe Gedankenreihe ſogleich wieder aufzunehmen, und die dazwiſchen liegenden Träume treten in weſenloſes Dunkel zurück. Eben ſo iſt es nun mit der dramatiſchen Darſtellung: unſre Einbildungskraft geht leicht über die Zeiten hinweg, welche vorausgeſetzt und angedeutet, aber weggelaſſen werden, weil nichts Bedeutendes darin vorgeht; ſie hält ſich einzig an die vorgeſtellten entſcheidenden Augenblicke, durch deren Zuſammendrängung der Dichter den trägen Gang der Stunden und Tage beflügelt."—SCHLEGEL, *Vorlesungen*, xviii.

IV.

22. "Je souhaiterois . . . que ce qu'on lui fait voir sur un théâtre qui ne change point pût s'arrêter dans une chambre ou dans une salle, suivant le choix qu'on en auroit fait: mais souvent cela est si malaisé, pour ne pas dire impossible, qu'il faut de nécessité trouver quelque élargissement pour le lieu comme pour le temps. . . .

"Je tiens donc qu'il faut chercher cette unité exacte autant qu'il est possible ; mais comme elle ne s'accommode pas avec toute sorte de sujets, j'accorderois très volontiers que ce qu'on feroit passer en une seule ville auroit l'unité de lieu. Ce n'est pas que je voulusse que le théâtre représentât cette ville toute entière, cela seroit un peu trop vaste, mais seulement deux ou trois lieux particuliers enfermés dans l'enclos de ses murailles."—CORNEILLE, *Troisième Discours.*

23. "Nous avons dit ailleurs que la mauvaise construction de nos théâtres, perpetuée depuis nos temps de barbarie jusqu'à nos jours, rendait la loi de l'unité de lieu presque impraticable. Les conjurés ne peuvent pas conspirer contre César dans sa chambre ; on ne s'entretient pas de ses intérêts secrets dans une place publique ; la même décoration ne peut représenter à la fois la façade d'un palais et celle d'un temple. **Il** faudrait **que** le théâtre fit voir **aux** yeux tous les endroits particuliers où la scène se passe, sans nuire à l'unité de lieu : ici, **une** partie d'un temple : là, le vestibule d'un palais ; une place publique, des rues dans l'enfoncement ; enfin tout ce qui est nécessaire pour montrer à l'œil tout ce que l'oreille doit entendre. L'unité de lieu est tout le spectacle que l'œil peut embrasser sans peine."—VOLTAIRE, *Remarques sur le Troisième Discours.*

24. "Passons à celle **de** l'unité de lieu, **qui ne** m'a pas moins donné de gêne **en cette** pièce. Je l'ai placé dans Séville, bien que Don Fernand n'en ait jamais été le maître ; et j'ai été obligé a cette falsification, pour former quelque vraisemblance à la déscente des Maures, dont l'armée ne pouvait **venir si** vite par terre que par eau. Je ne voudrois pas assurer toutefois que le flux de la mer monte effectivement jusque-là ; mais comme dans notre Seine il fait encore plus de chemin qu'il ne lui en faut faire sur le Guadalquivir pour battre les murailles de cette ville, cela peut suffire à fonder quelque probabilité parmi nous, pour ceux qui n'ont pas été sur le lieu même. . . .

"Tout s'y passe donc dans Séville, et garde ainsi quelque espèce d'unité de lieu en général ; mais le lieu particulier change de **scène en** scène, et tantôt c'est le palais du roi, tantôt l'appartement de l'infante, tantôt la maison de Chimène, et tantôt une rue ou place publique. On le détermine aisément pour les scènes détachées ; mais pour celles qui ont leur liaison ensemble, comme les quatre dernières du premier acte, il est malaisé d'en choisir un qui convienne à toutes. Le Comte et Don Diègue se querellent au sortir du palais ;

cela se peut passer dans une rue : mais, après le soufflet reçu, Don Diègue ne peut pas demeurer dans cette rue à faire ses plaintes, en attendant que son fils survienne, qu'il ne soit tout aussitôt environné de peuple, et ne reçoive l'offre de quelques amis. Ainsi il seroit plus à propos qu'il se plaignît dans sa maison, où le met l'Espagnol, pour laisser aller ses sentiments en liberté ; mais en ce cas il faudroit délier les scènes comme il a fait. En l'état où elles sont ici, on peut dire qu'il faut quelquefois aider au théâtre, et suppléer favorablement ce qui ne s'y peut représenter. ₊Deux personnes s'y arrêtent pour parler, et quelquefois il faut présumer qu'ils marchent, ce qu'on ne peut exposer sensiblement à la vue, parcequ'ils échapperoient aux yeux avant que d'avoir pu dire ce qu'il est nécessaire qu'ils fassent savoir à l'auditeur. Ainsi, par une fiction de théâtre, on peut s'imaginer que Don Diègue et le Comte, sortant du palais du roi, avancent toujours en se querellant, et sont arrivés devant la maison de ce premier lorsqu'il reçoit le soufflet qui l'oblige à y entrer pour y chercher du secours. Si cette fiction poétique ne vous satisfait point, laissons le dans la place publique, et disons que le concours du peuple autour de lui après cette offense, et les offres de service que lui font les premiers amis qui s'y rencontrent, sont des circonstances que le roman ne doit pas oublier, mais que ces menues actions ne servant de rien à la principale, il n'est pas besoin que le poëte s'en embarasse sur la scène."—CORNEILLE, *Examen du " Cid."*

25. " Pour le lieu, bien que l'unité y soit exacte, elle n'est pas sans quelque contrainte. Il est constant qu'Horace et Camille n'ont point de raison de se separer du reste de la famille pour commencer le second acte ; et c'est une adresse de théâtre de n'en donner aucune, quand on n'en peut donner de bonnes. L'attachement de l'auditeur à l'action présente souvent ne lui permet pas de descendre à l'examen sévère de cette justesse, et ce n'est pas un crime de s'en prévaloir pour

l'éblouir, quand il est malaisé de le satisfaire."—CORNEILLE, *Examen d'Horace.*

26. ## SCÈNE III.

ARONS., **ALBIN.**

(Qui sont supposés être entrés de la salle d'audience dans un autre appartement de la maison de Brutus.)

27. "Le cabinet où était Semiramis fait place à un grand salon magnifiquement orné."

28. "Pour rectifier en quelque façon cette duplicité de lieu, quand elle est inevitable, je voudrois qu'on fît deux choses ; l'une, que jamais on **ne** changeât dans le même acte, mais seulement de l'un à l'autre, comme il **se** fait dans **les** trois premiers de Cinna."—CORNEILLE, *Troisième Discours.*

29. "L'entr'acte est une absence des acteurs **et** des specta-teurs. **Les acteurs** peuvent donc **avoir** changé de lieu d'un acte **à** l'autre ; et les spectateurs n'ayant point de lieu fixe, ils sont partout où se passe l'action : si elle change de lieu, ils changent avec elle. Ce qui doit être vraisemblable, c'est que l'action ait pu se déplacer ; et pour cela il faut un inter-valle. Ce n'est donc presque jamais d'une scène à l'autre, mais seulement d'un acte à l'autre, que peut s'opérer le changement de lieu. **Je** sais bien que pour le faciliter au milieu d'un acte on peut rompre l'enchaînement des **scènes** et laisser le théâtre vide un instant ; mais **cet instant ne** suffirait point **à la** vraisemblance, surtout si les mêmes **acteurs** qu'on vient de voir passaient incontinent **dans** le nouveau lieu **de** la scène. Après tout, **ce** n'est pas trop gêner les poëtes, que d'exiger d'eux à la rigueur l'unité de lieu pour chaque acte, avec la possibilité **morale** du passage d'un lieu à un autre dans l'intervalle supposé."—MARMONTEL, *Élé-**ments** de Littérature. Art. "Unites."*

V.

30. „In gedachter Vorrede erklärt er ferner ohne Hehl, daß er sich von den strengen Bedingungen der Zeit und des Ortes lossage, führt August Wilhelm Schlegels Aeußerungen hierüber als entscheidend an, und zeigt die Nachtheile der bisherigen, ängstlich beschränkten Behandlung. Hier findet freilich der Deutsche nur das bekannte, ihm begegnet nichts, dem er widersprechen möchte; allein die Bemerkungen des Herrn Manzoni sind dennoch aller Aufmerksamkeit auch bei uns werth. Denn obgleich diese Angelegenheit in Deutschland lange genug durchgesprochen und durchgefochten worden, so findet doch ein geistreicher Mann, der eine gute Sache aufs Neue, unter andern Umständen, zu vertheidigen angeregt wird, immer wieder eine frische Seite, von der sie zu betrachten und zu billigen ist, und sucht die Argumente der Gegner mit neuen Gründen zu entkräften und zu widerlegen; wie denn der Verfasser einiges anbringt, welches den gemeinen Menschenverstand anlächelt, und selbst dem schon Ueberzeugten wohlgefällt."—GOETHE, *Il Conte di Carmagnola*, Bd. 25.

31. "Tra i vani espedienti che gli uomini hanno trovati per imbrogliarisi reciprocamente, uno dei più ingegnosi è quello d'avere, quasi per ogni argomento, due massime opposte, tenute egualmente per infallibili. Applicando quest' uso anche ai piccoli interessi della poesia, essi dicono a chi la esercita, 'Siate originali, e non fate nulla di cui i grandi poeti non vi abbiano lasciato l' esempio.' Questi commandi che rendono difficile l' arte più di quello che è gia, levano anche a un scrittore la speranza di poter rendere ragione d' un lavoro poetico. . . . L' unità di luogo, e la cosi detta unità di tempo, non sono regole fondate nella ragione dell' arte, nè connaturali all' indole del poema drammatico, ma sono venute da una autorità non bene intesa, e da principi arbitrari. . . .

"Finalmente queste regole impediscono molte bellezze, e producono molti inconvenienti."—ALLESSANDRO MANZONI, *Prefazione al " Conte di Carmagnola."*

32. "Ce qu'il y a d'étrange, c'est que les routiniers prétendent appuyer leur règle des deux unités sur la vraisemblance, tandis que c'est précisement le réel qui la tue. Quoi de plus invraisemblable **et** de plus absurde en effet que ce vestibule, **ce** péristyle, cette antichambre, lieu banal où nos tragédies **ont la** complaisance **de venir se** dérouler ; où arrivent, **on ne sait** comment, les conspirateurs pour déclamer **contre** le tyran, le tyran pour déclamer contre les conspirateurs, chacun à leur tour, comme s'ils s'étaient dit bucoliquement—

" 'Alternis cantemus ; amant alterna Camenæ.'

. . . . "L'unité de temps n'est pas plus solide que l'unité de lieu. L'action encadrée de force dans les vingt-quatre heures est aussi ridicule qu'encadrée dans le vestibule. Toute action a sa durée propre comme son lieu particulier. Verser la même dose de temps à **tous** les événements ! On rizait d'un cordonnier qui voudrait mettre le même soulier à tous les pieds. Croiser l'unité de temps **à** l'unité de lieu comme les barreaux d'une cage, et y faire pedantesquement entrer, de **par** Aristote, **tous** ces faits, tous ces peuples, toutes ces figures que la Providence déroule à si grandes masses dans la réalité ! C'est mutiler hommes et choses, c'est faire grimacer l'histoire. Disons mieux ; tout cela mourra dans l'opération ; et c'est ainsi que les mutilateurs dogmatiques arrivent à leur resultat ordinaire ; ce qui étai vivant dans la chronique, c'est mort dans la tragédie. Voila pourquoi, bien souvent, la cage des unités ne renferme qu'une squelette. Et puis si vingt-quatre heures peuvent être comprises dans deux, il serait logique que quatre heures puissent en contenir quarante-huit. L'unité de Shakespeare **ne** sera donc pas l'unité **de** Corneille. Pitié ! ce sont là pourtant les pauvres **chicanes** que depuis deux siècles la médiocrité, l'envi, et la **routine** font au genié ! C'est ainsi qu'on a borné l'essor **de** nos plus grandes poètes. C'est avec les ciseaux des unités qu'on leur a coupé l'aile. Et que nous a-t-on donné en échange de ces plumes d'aigle retranchées à Corneille et à Racine? Campistron !—Victor Hugo, "*Preface to Cromwell.*"

33. „Denn auch durch eine solche Unterbrechung der dramatischen Handlung wird auf der Griechischen Bühne bis zu einem gewissen Grade das erreicht, was die dramatischen Dichter aller Zeiten durch den Decorationswechsel, das heißt, durch die Aufhebung der Einheit des Raums, hervorgebracht haben; sie unterbrechen damit für das Gefühl des Zuschauers zugleich die Continuität der Zeit, heben sie auf, und gewinnen statt der durch Reflection meßbaren die für das Drama unentbehrliche incommensurable, ideale Zeit. Mag nun Dikaiopolis auch noch brummend über das, was eben in der Volksversammlung geschehen ist, wieder auftreten, mag ihn auch der rückkehrende Amphitheos mitten in diesem Gebrumme unterbrechen, das schadet nicht; während des Scenenwechsels hat dieser doch die Zeit gehabt, die Reise nach Sparta hin und zurück zu machen. Man sehe nur nach —— bei dem größten Meister aller dramatischen Kunst, bei dem Dichter, der das feinste Gefühl, ich möchte sagen, den angebornen Instinct grade für Bühnenwirkung hat, wie kein Anderer (wenigstens wie kein neuerer Dichter —ich denke, indem ich dies hinzusetze, an Aischylos, namentlich an die wundervolle Kunst, mit der er im Agamemnon die Zeit aufgehoben und dem Hörer das Berechnen unmöglich gemacht hat): also bei Shakespeare wird man Hunderte von Beispielen finden dafür, daß nach einem Decorationswechsel die nächste Scene sich auf der einen Seite ganz unmittelbar an die eben vorhergegangene anschließt, und daß doch sogleich etwas eintritt, was das Verfließen einer längeren Zeit während der Verwandlung voraussetzt."—MÜLLER STRÜBING, *Aristophanes*, p. 695.

34. „Es kommt darauf an, fuhr Goethe fort, daß Sie sich ein Capital bilden, das nie ausgeht. Dieses werden Sie erlangen in dem begonnenen Studium der englischen Sprache und Literatur. Halten Sie sich dazu und benutzen Sie die treffliche Gelegenheit der jungen Engländer zu jeder Stunde. Die alten Sprachen sind Ihnen in der Jugend größtentheils

entgangen, deßhalb suchen Sie in der Literatur **einer so tüchtigen**
Nation, wie die Engländer, **einen** Halt. Indem **ist** ja **unsere**
eigene Literatur größtentheils aus der ihrigen hergekommen.
Unsere Romane, unsere Trauerspiele, woher haben wir **sie**
denn: als von Goldschmidt, Fielding **und** Shakspeare? **Und**
noch heut zu Tage, **wo** wollen Sie denn **in** Deutschland drei
literarische **Helden** finden, die dem Lord Byron, Moore **und**
Walter Scott an die Seite zu setzen wären? Also noch einmal,
befestigen Sie sich im Englischen, halten Sie Ihre Kräfte zu etwas
Tüchtigem zusammen und lassen Sie alles fahren, was für Sie
keine Folge hat und Ihnen nicht gemäß ist."—*Gespräche mit*
Eckermann, 3ten December 1824.

35. „Goethe gab mir Recht und lachte über Lord Byron,
daß er, der sich im Leben **nie** gefügt und **der** nie nach einem
Gesetz gefragt, sich endlich dem dümmsten Gesetz der drei Einheiten unterworfen habe. „**Er hat** den Grund dieses Gesetzes
so wenig verstanden, sagte er, als die übrige Welt. Das Faßliche **ist der** Grund, und die drei Einheiten **sind** nur in so fern
gut, **als** dieses durch sie erreicht wird. Sind **sie** aber dem
Faßlichen hinderlich, so ist es immer unverständig sie als Gesetz
betrachten und befolgen zu wollen. Selbst die Griechen, von
denen diese Regel ausging, haben sie nicht immer befolgt; im
Phaëthon des Euripides und in anderen Stücken wechselt der
Ort, und man sieht also, daß die gute Darstellung ihres Gegen-
standes ihnen mehr galt, als der blinde Respect vor einem Gesetz,
das an sich nie viel zu bedeuten hatte. Die Shakspear'schen
Stücke gehen über **die** Einheit der Zeit und **des** Orts so weit
hinaus, als nur möglich; aber sie sind faßlich, **es ist** nichts
faßlicher als sie, und deßhalb würden auch die Griechen sie
untadelig finden. Die französischen Dichter haben dem
Gesetz **der** drei Einheiten **am** strengsten Folge zu leisten gesucht,
aber **Sie** sündigen gegen das Faßliche, indem Sie ein dra-
matisches Gesetz nicht dramatisch lösen, sondern durch Erzählung."
—ECKERMANN, *Gespräche mit Göthe,* 1825.

REVIEWS.

"THE phrase, 'Dramatic Unities,' is one which, we fancy, is occasionally used by writers without exact comprehension of all that is implied by that once potent formula, and when there is a disposition among dramatic critics to revive it, as, according to Mr Simpson, is the case at present in England, it is only proper that their claim should be carefully considered. For this purpose this little volume will be found to be admirably fitted. It quotes from Aristotle the passages which are assumed to be the basis of the theory, and at the same time points out their application in the work of Gian Giorgio Trissino, one of the court of Leo X., and later writers. It is shown that the Greek tragedians did not comply with the laws afterwards promulgated from their plays; and there follows an excellent summary of the arguments on the matter, with quotations from the French critics who supported it, and from Schlegel, Lessing, Göthe, and Dr Johnson on the other side. There are also admirable illustrations of the difficulties of exact compliance with the rules enforced upon the French tragedians. Statistics are given of the efforts of English playwrights to cut themselves free from all the traditions of their wonderful dramatic literature, and to fashion their work after the requirements of unnatural laws. As the matter now stands, it would seem to be beginning at the wrong end to attempt to reform the defective play-writing of the present day, by imposing novel and difficult rules upon a class of authors who are for the most part incapable of rising above abject triviality. The general principle we can look at with great equanimity; the battle has been fought, and the absolute power of the dramatic unities has been broken, but there is no one who would condemn a good play because the author had chosen to observe them. To demand them, however—to insist on them—is a very different and a most mischievous thing. One might as well ask of our artists that they paint nothing but Madonnas. How small is the foundation on which the theory rests is clearly and temperately shown in this little book. We hope it may be read, if for no other purpose than to see how a pretentious and bastard formula can impose for a long time on literature."—*New York Nation.*

"The only fault of Mr Simpson's clever and instructive book upon the unities is that it comes a day too late for the fair. In England, and indeed throughout the Continent, the unities, those of place and time, by which alone the drama is repressed, are abandoned. If the unity of action still survives, it is in a form very different from that assigned it in the time of Corneille. So far as it holds a place at all, it is axiomatic in truth ; and those who fight its wider application are fighting a shadow. In bringing together all the authorities on the subject, in giving a history of the growth and decay of faith in the unities, and in showing their influence upon dramatic art, Mr Simpson supplies a treatise useful to students, and contributes an interesting chapter to literature. He is careful in advancing his authorities. Messrs Trübner & Co. are the publishers."—*Athenæum.*

"A volume on the dramatic unities is something of a surprise in these days, in which all questions concerning them might fairly be supposed to be dismissed. 'An apparent inclination on the part of some of our leading dramatic critics to revive the old doctrines of the unities of time and place' has induced Mr Simpson to publish a volume which contains at once a condemnation of the use of the unities and a history of their rise and growth. Without stopping to inquire whom the cap fits, or to ask whether there is, indeed, in reference to the unities in theatrical criticism, any intention more serious than that of airing a little erudition, we may say at once that the publication of a short but comprehensive treatise upon the unities is a boon to all concerned with or interested in dramatic history. Ask a moderately well-informed man what are the unities ? and it is a chance whether he can tell you anything about them. Most probably he will assert they have something to do with the time over which the action of a play may extend, and will add that they are an invention of Aristotle. General readers will be thankful for information upon a subject on which they are assumably ignorant, and will be glad to be put in a position to understand the frequent references which are made to them in disquisitions upon theatrical subjects. The best way to obtain full information is, of course, to turn to the book. This is the course we recommend to all whose interest in the question is deep. For those, however, whom a smattering of information will satisfy, we proceed to dissect Mr Simpson's work. Aristotle is, of course, so far responsible for the unities that warrant for them is drawn from his 'Poetics.' Minds not accustomed to deductions of this class are a little at a loss to know how far the premises warrant the conclusion. The works of Aristotle are indeed in this respect like Holy Writ, seeing that men of the most contrary and conflicting opinions may find justification for their respective views. Some words in the 'Poetics' suggest the unities of time as having been aimed at by tragedians. The unity of place is, however, as difficult to evolve from Aristotle as Dr Cumming's notions of the often postponed end of the world taken from the Apocalypse.

"The unities are supposed to be three—those of time, place, and action. The last of these may be speedily dismissed. What Aristotle meant is but imperfectly understood, and critics have written pages of learned rubbish upon it. So far as it can be shown to mean anything, it means what every one will admit, that the action must be clear and progressive, that minor intrigues must be subordinated to the principal motive, and that the characters should be consistent. The unity of time is the most important and the most oppressive. Aristotle, drawing a distinction between the tragedy and the epos, says 'tragedy attempts, as far as possible, to restrict itself to a single revolution of the sun, or to exceed it but little, whereas the epos is indefinite as

regards time, and in this respect differs (from tragedy).'
Upon this notion the advocates of the unities determined
that the action of a serious play must not exceed twenty-
four hours, which Corneille extended to thirty. Some
profound sticklers for orthodoxy went further than this, and
maintained that a play to be regular in construction and
worthy of praise must take in presentation exactly the time
which the real events would require for their accomplishment. From this rule to that expressing the unity of place
was a natural transition. By this third of the unities the
action must continue where it began. A spectator must not,
as in our Shaksperian plays, be in London in one scene and,
it may be, in Salisbury or in Paris in the next. At the
same time, as a too rigid adherence to the room in which
the story commenced would bring about absurdities and
improbabilities much more offensive than those it was
intended to remove, Corneille, the great adherent to the
unities, fixed the limits of a town as those the dramatist
might not overpass. Having now briefly told what are the
unities, we may give Mr Simpson's account of their origin.
They were first heard of at the court of Leo X., and are to
be ascribed to the influence of the revived taste for classical
literature manifested in Italy during the period of the
ascendancy of the Medici. 'Directly,' says Mr Simpson,
'their invention or revival is traceable to one of the most
gifted members of that gifted assemblage (the court of Leo
X.)—namely, Gian Giorgio Trissino.' This is so far true
that the 'Sofonisba' of Trissino is built upon the model of
ancient tragedy, the form of which it copies with an almost
servile spirit of imitation. That Trissino mentioned the
unities by name does not appear. He is, however, certainly
entitled to the credit of having set an example, which followed, first by his countrymen, then extended to France,
Germany, Holland, and Northern Europe, exercised for a
couple of centuries the most baneful influence upon the
drama of half the civilised world, crippling that of France,
and choking that of other countries wherein the dramatic
spirit was less powerful to bear up against its burdens. Spain

and England it practically scarcely reached. While, accordingly, for centuries the drama languished elsewhere under classical trammels, Spain and England produced a thoroughly national and vigorous drama, which anticipated by more than two centuries the freedom French writers subsequently won. During the seventeenth and eighteenth centuries French dramatists consented to be bound by their rulers, and French critics extolled them to the skies. The drama of England and Spain, known as the romantic drama, was treated as barbarous, and the productions of Shakespeare were pronounced the works of an inspired madman. About the third decade of the present century the appearance of a band of young writers brought a change. After a fierce fight, in which the new school was led by men like Victor Hugo, Alexandre Dumas, De Musset and De Vigny among poets, and Sainte Beuve and Theophile Gautier among critics, for the poems of the latter come later, and those of the former **are** of little account, the old school was defeated and the unities were relegated **to** the limbo of vanities.

"**It** is useless to dwell long upon the absurdity of these rules **as** binding in **art.** In England we have always, until a few years ago, when the national spirit first began to give signs of sleepiness, kicked against unnecessary restrictions. ' Thus, though there are a few plays written in conformity with the unities, not one of them preserves its position as an acting play, and none can claim to be counted among the works of which an Englishman is proud. There is, of course, something to be said in favour of the idea on which they are based. Few notions that have exercised a strong influence over the minds of many men are wholly without **value.** When an action can pass without frequent change of scene, and within the limits of a given and probable time, it is, of course, easy to accept. The effort, however, to bring arbitrarily action within certain limits produces always results more preposterous than would accrue under any excesses of imagination on the part of the spectator. No play written in conformity with the unities enjoys a higher reputation than 'The Cid' of Corneille. In order to bring the action of this play within the range of time he fixes—namely, thirty hours—Corneille presents the following things as occurring within that space of time. First, we see the Cid obscure, as yet winning the favour of the heroine ; next we see him challenging the first soldier of Spain for an insult to his father and slaying him. Then, after a considerable space spent in lovemaking and listening to the rebukes of Ximena and debates as to what punishment, if any, is to be administered, he fights a desperate battle against the Moors, conquers them, and brings in their monarchs captive. Even now his labours are not ended. He has to hear the compliments of the King, make love again, fight another duel, and at length win back the avowal of the love of Ximena. The spectator simply refuses to accept any such sequence as possible within the space. Equal difficulty attends the unity of time. A spectator can as easily be transferred from Italy to Egypt as he can from England to Italy. There is, however, no need to fight shadows which these once formidable unities have now become. It is, however, just to say that in one respect English dramatists now submit to a restriction for which these things are in part—though only in part—responsible. The unities of time and place seem now to circumscribe the act. Most acts in a new play have one scene only, and the time never exceeds twenty-four hours. Such a rule as this, however, is only to be regarded while it remains convenient. No genuine playgoer ever felt the changes of scene in 'As You Like It' disturb for one moment his enjoyment. When discussing this subject it is but just to Mr Simpson to say that his industry and cleverness of view are equally to be commended. From all sources — Greek, Latin, Italian, French, German, and English—he has gathered every scrap of information bearing upon his subject. He writes clearly, convincingly, and well. The result is a book which, while to the critic it is an invaluable little manual, is fruitful to the general reader both of pleasure and instruction."—*Sunday Times.*

www.ingramcontent.com/pod-product-compliance
Lightning Source LLC
Chambersburg PA
CBHW032145010726
47493CB00008BA/2583